Fall From Grace

Alan Feldberg

BLOODHOUND
— BOOKS —

First published in 2024 by Bloodhound Books.

www.bloodhoundbooks.com

Print ISBN: 978-1-916978-48-5

*This book is dedicated to my daughters,
both of whom live and breathe in it.*

Chapter One
Now

A room feels different when there is a dead person in it. It feels like a place you don't belong. Like you're witnessing something you have no right to. It becomes a shameful place.

I'm sitting on the bed. It is a high bed. Why do old people always have such high beds? Is it the bed that's high or do they just double up the mattresses? I had to look over my shoulder and do a little backwards hop to get up here. My feet don't even touch the floor.

It's not my bed. It belongs to Doris. She is the dead person in the room. She is sitting in the chair by the window. In my head she's always been Flo, and I've always called her Flo. She thinks that it's quite common to give some people names that aren't their own, names that feel like they fit better. She thinks it's because we knew them by that name in another life. It makes sense. If you believe in reincarnation. I've not decided on that yet.

I can't tell you how old Flo is. She is of an age to have a high bed. Haha. And her eyes weep from the outer corners, not the inner ones. I think that's a sign of advancing years, too. There isn't anyone else here. It's just us. Does she count? She's been dead for hours. I said hello when I came in, boiled the kettle for some tea and came and sat down on the chair beside her. The large bay windows look out over the street onto the ocean. When it's windy, as it is today, we sit and watch the breeze blowing the tops off the waves breaking shallow on the beach. Far out on the horizon it looks like it might be raining. There are great, grey clouds tumbling over each other. If I could walk on water, as once I thought I could, I wonder if I could walk out to them or if they'd remain as far away as they are now.

I stare at the back of Flo's head, the top half of it sticking out above the high-backed chair. Her hair is thin. I can see right through it to her scalp, where there is a wart, bright pink against the pale, almost fluorescent white of her skin. The wart is all bunched at the top, like it's being drawn down a hole in the middle. I think irreverently of a baboon's arse. I get a sudden urge to walk up behind her and squeeze it. The idea repulses me. My dog had warts. Whatever came out of them stained his fur the colour of a muddy puddle and when I patted him I was always careful to steer clear. Sometimes I misjudged it and my fingers would bump over one of these growths. I'd have to rub him vigorously somewhere else then. Somewhere where he was smooth. He'd think it was love. But really I was wiping my hands on him.

I hop off the bed and resume the chair opposite hers. Her eyes are open and they reflect in bulbous miniature the scene beyond the window. I lean in closer. I'm looking to see if I can spot seagulls in reverse. I can't. Only three tankers that seem to be hovering in space.

'What should I do now?' I ask.

She always has good advice to give. She told me once to save all my positive energy for the people closest to me, not to waste it on the rest. It seems simple, but it carries a lot of weight when you think about it longer.

'Flo? Should I call someone? Your son?'

I pick up the phone and dial. I listen to it ringing on the other end. I'm just about to hang up when someone answers. It's a girl. She sounds young. She asks if she can help me. I don't answer at first and she asks again. Eventually I say, 'Can I place an order for delivery, please?'

It's evening now and I am back in my own flat. I am in my own chair. It is night and the tankers are orange lights twinkling out of the blackness. The empty pizza box is on the carpet next to the empty dog's bed. No one can see me here, my hands limp in my lap, a smear of barbeque sauce down my shirt. I'll wear this shirt tomorrow. And the day after that. Who can stop me? No one can. That's who. I look again at the lights of the tankers. I hear the wind drumming the pane. The seas will be high and stormy out there but the lights don't seem to move. I stare at them until they blur then double.

I am thinking of someone else now, as I always do at this time of night. A dozen images, two dozen, arrive at once. I am not sure if they are the moments themselves or the pictures I took of them. And then that last image. She is nine years old. She is watching from her window – was it her? – as I duck into the car.

I blink and the lights of the tankers come back into focus. I look over at my bed. It seems so far way. I sink a little deeper into the cushions. She will be a teenager now. I don't believe it. At some undefined point I will fall asleep in this chair. When I wake up it will be 1,847 days since I last saw her. They are both gone from me.

Chapter Two
Then

I am in the middle of a wood not far from where I work. I am bent double, rummaging beneath low-hanging branches. Every now and then my rump bumps a tree and its leaves shake a load of freezing rainwater on me. In this position it streams under my collar and down my spine, making me shiver. Sometimes I swear. Sometimes I just think about swearing.

I love it here really. Often I'll come here during my lunch hour because I know there is no chance of bumping into anyone I know. I don't have to do much when I get here, to make it worth my while. I'll usually just kick the leaves about, enjoying the fact that I'm alone and won't be disturbed. There are all sorts of trees here. I don't know their names. Some of them carry their thick plumage all year round. There is a word for trees like this. Is it evergreen? Can it really be as self-explanatory as that? There are bare trees here too. They are stark and jagged in comparison. Almost deformed-looking. Their exposed branches jerk in the wind, clawing at the sky like arthritic fingers. Coniferous. It pops into my head just like that.

Today I have a purpose though. I am on a special mission. It's for Grace. Most everything I do is. She has been fretting lately. About school and other things – who knows exactly what bright nine-year-olds fret about. I want to find her a piece of wood. That's my mission. Not just any piece of wood. It needs to be just right. I don't know what just right will look like, but I'll know it when I see it.

It's been raining all morning. The earth is sodden and sucks my shoes down with each step. They squelch when I lift them again. I imagine the state I'll be in when I return to work, when I walk past their desks to my own. Dragging behind me something that could easily be mistaken for a club. I see the stares. Perhaps they'll worry I'll use it on them. *Before he turned the weapon on himself.* But I'm not that person.

There is a dog here now. Where did he come from? He is at my heels. He is playful, but also a little uncertain. Like me, he probably thinks this is his territory. I look up. A woman is nearby. She isn't coming any closer. She is hiding beneath a hood.

'Hello,' I say. I say it cheerfully and deliver a smile with it.

She whistles quickly and the dog hurries after her as she walks away. There! There! That's it! Just what I was after. I knew I'd know it. It is smooth and bone white and just the right thickness. Its knuckles and gnarls lend it a certain mystical charm. It's perfect. Only it is the middle part of a much longer branch. I lean down and tug at it and more of it stirs beneath the foliage. It must be all of ten feet. At one end it fans out and thin fingers entangle themselves in other trees. But this is for Grace. There are no lengths. I want this branch and only this branch. I plan to make it into something special that will magic away my daughter's fears. And I won't be denied. I begin dragging the entire thing through the wood. Finally I get it into the open. By wedging it into a farmer's gate and jumping on its middle I manage to break it down to the solid mid-section. It is still longer than my arm, but I can whittle it down further at home. For now, this will have to do.

It is evening now. Quite late. Grace is asleep. It was just her and me tonight. I made her favourite dinner. Takeaway. Haha. Dolores is away. Another work trip. Where is it this time? She did tell me. Frankfurt? Cologne? Yes, Cologne. I made stupid jokes about smelling an opportunity and being on the scent of money. She stared at me dead-eyed. I don't mind really. Her job matters to her. And she's good at it. At least I assume she is. Why else would they fly her all around the world? By they I mean he.

I slip out the front door and retrieve the branch from my boot. Yes. Much too long. I come back inside and start searching for a saw even though I know we don't have one. Have never had one. I look in all the kitchen cupboards and drawers. I look in that black hole beneath the stairs. I go out into the back garden and walk around the perimeter. Why? I don't own a saw. I know I don't. I'm not my father. I see him now bent over the workbench. Something is in a vice. What was he making, or fixing?

I return to the kitchen and unsheathe a breadknife from the wooden block. I put my thumb against the blade. It is sharp but flimsy. It will have to do. I put the branch in the sink and begin to cut. An hour passes. It feels like an hour. I take the branch out and examine my progress. Lack of. I get a screwdriver – I still have one of those – and hammer it through the branch. I take the branch outside and bang it against the wall. The shock jars my elbow. I'm not as robust as I was. I return to the kitchen and pick up the knife again. No, I won't be denied.

I start thinking that I must be the best dad in the world.

Nay, parent. The things I do. Other dads would give up. Or not even start. They can't be bothered. But I bother. I don't mind the hardships. Each one separates me from them.

Eventually I manage to cut through the branch. I scrub it clean and put it on the radiator to dry. Then I sit down and begin writing a letter with my left hand.

It is morning now. I don't know what time. Early. Grace is here. She woke me up by jumping on me.

'Oomph,' I said, rolling onto my side, away from her.

'Wake up, Daddy! Wake up! I have news!'

She clambers off the bed and even with my head under the pillow I see the light come on.

'Too bright,' I say.

Her weight lands back on the bed and I feel her little hands on my shoulders through the blanket as she starts shaking me. I remain limp. I start snoring.

'I know you're awake, Daddy, you've already spoken to me.'

I emerge from beneath the pillow and look at her. Grace is not a pretty child. Worse than that, she is very nearly ugly. Her eyes are too small and her nose and mouth are pinched and thin. There is, altogether, not enough feature and too much face. I hate to acknowledge this fact, even privately. I wonder about the pain it will cause her as she gets older and these things start to matter more. Children can be so nasty. But they grew up so fast these days. Perhaps it has already started.

'What's up, my friend? What news?'

She holds the section of branch I made and the letter I wrote. She is smiling. That's not a big enough word. She is tired, there are dark shadows under her eyes – she hasn't slept well for such a long time – but she is fully beaming at me. I savour her

7

expression. I did that. I think of the muddy work shoes. The soaked shirt. Being up till all hours. I don't care about any of that. This is why I bother.

'They wrote to me, Daddy!'

'Did they?' I rub my eyes and act out a great yawn. It turns into a real one. 'Who did?'

'Here,' she says, 'I'll read it to you:

'Dear Grace,

It was lovely to receive your letter. We do enjoy reading them so much. But I'm sorry you have been worried. I would like to say don't worry. Remember, we are magic and have special powers. We can see things that humans can't, and we know that in the end you are going to be very happy. But in the meantime, we want to give you this. It is one of our special benches. It has been in the fairy kingdom for more than a thousand years. I can't imagine how many of us have sat on it in that time! It is one of the benches we go to when we have problems to solve or unhappys to make happy again. I am sure that some of our good feelings must have gone into the wood by now – it's a living thing, after all – so perhaps, if you hold it in your hand when you are worried it will help you to relax. We hope so. Because you are our favourite human. Remember, we are always nearby, watching over you.

Love, Chantal, Queen of all the Fairies.'

When Grace stops reading she looks up at me.

'See?' she says.

'I do,' I answer, nodding gravely. 'I do.'

She looks at the wood. Holds it up to her too-small nose and smells it. 'Don't tell anyone else, Daddy. This must always be a secret.'

Chapter Three
Now

I 'm on the landing outside Flo's door. Her pot plants are gathered expectantly at my feet. I can hear them. I'm sure I can. Please, sir, we want some more. They will die now. Without her. But I'm not sure. Did all that really happen? I woke up bent in my chair. Just where I left myself last night. I stayed there. I gazed blankly at the sky beyond the window. I unfolded myself, painfully, cranking my body upright, and came here. I put my fingertips against her door and tap.

'Flo?'

Softly at first. Then a little louder. Nothing stirs in there. I grip the handle and twist. I just need to push and all will be revealed. My hand stops twisting. It lets go and the latch springs back into place. I turn away and walk down the stairs. Life goes on. For me it does.

The beach really is just a stone's throw away. Other people say that but they don't really mean it. So why say it? It makes me doubt everything about them. At this time of morning the tide is out and the water's edge is hundreds of yards away. That's not even an exaggeration. The sand is hard and wet and ribbed. I look down at it and squint. It looks like a desert. Seen from a plane window. It hurts my bare feet as I walk.

I made a mistake. Not going in there. That was poor form. She is my friend, after all. Was. Am I ready to say that? I think of the first time we met. Met is too strong a word for it. I was lugging my mattress up the stairs. It didn't want to go. It was fighting back. Shoving me against the wall and wrapping itself up in the rail. Perhaps it knew what would happen up there and wanted no part of it. Flo was at the top, watering her plants. She was always there after that. Never when I left. Always when I returned. It took me a long time to realise she went out there to wait for me, that our little nods and hellos were the only human contact she had.

The buttons of her cardigan were one out. That first time. It created a disturbing fold in the material. I wanted to be away from it. I couldn't comprehend how she could stand it. I'd like now to attribute more meaning to that first moment. She caught my eye and something about the look we exchanged... She said hello and immediately I realised... There was none of that. I noticed her without noticing her. Like how you realise in hindsight that you saw someone who would become important to you before they did, when they were still just strangers.

I look back across the sand towards the row of houses leaning distastefully over the beachfront. Ours among them. Are they Georgian? Someone said they were. Who did? What era is Georgian? But wait, I don't care. I look at her window. Just below the chimney with the nest. There are chicks in there now. She will be sitting directly behind the glass. You'd never know it. Not with her window so full of sun. Like they all are. I lift my arm and wave. Then quickly lower it and continue on.

The water isn't even cold. I wade straight out up to my chest then take a deep breath and sink under. I do this every single morning. The weather to stop me hasn't yet been discovered. I'd like to stop. Like a normal person would. I'd much prefer to stay cupped for hours in the deep cushions of my chair. One morning I got up and came down here, I can't remember why, and now I'm compelled. I don't even fight it anymore. I sit on the seabed for as long as I can, eyes squeezed shut and holding my nose. How do people kill themselves this way? I really can't fathom it. Virginia Woolf managed. Many more besides. How did they force themselves to stay under when the air ran out? When the surface was just there? How did they resist the life-pull to just stand up and gulp the air? Rocks in their pockets. That's the answer. But they could have just taken them out again. It's not that I don't understand the suicide instinct. I just don't understand this method. Tablets. A gun. Even jumping off a great height or in front of a train. That way you can't back out. Once you make the decision and start the act, it's irrevocable, requiring no further effort on your part. Drowning, I imagine, must be like shooting yourself with a bullet that travels a millimetre a second. How do you not withdraw your temple?

Yes, I made a mistake not going in there. But this time I don't hesitate. I open her door and walk straight in without missing a beat. She hasn't moved overnight. Obviously.

'Morning, Flo. Tea? No? Just for me then.'

I boil the kettle then take my seat beside her. This is our spot. Here in front of the bay windows. All this natural light. The hours, days, salad days, we must have whiled away here.

'Look at the sky today. Isn't it marvellous? Why do you think it seems so much further away some days than others? It looks miles up there now. Don't you think? Like it's right on the edge of space.'

I'm waffling, of course. Nervous excitement. I'm not sure I've seen a dead body before. I'm racking my brain. I seem to remember an old boy laid out in a coffin, thick white hair, white moustache that covered his mouth and made him look like a cowboy to my young eyes – I know I was young because when I approached the coffin I had to stand on tiptoes to see over its edge. Maybe that really happened, maybe not.

I've seen the dead bodies of animals though. I am certain of that. I once ran over a dog. It came bounding out from between parked cars and was bumping beneath the chassis before it knew what... I nearly said before it knew what hit it. But it never knew. Its owner rushed out and I see myself standing in the road looking at him holding the stricken beast in his arms. It wasn't quite dead yet, but blood was spooling out its mouth. I ran over a rabbit once, too. That time it was deliberate. It was already injured in some way, panting in a gutter and covered in ants. I could hardly leave it to its drawn-out fate. Then I killed a dying gerbil with a brick, and clubbed the life out of a badger that had been mauled by a fox or a dog or an uncivilised boy. This must make me sound slightly cruel. It was the opposite of cruelty each time. Apart from the dog. But each time after that it was only mercy that made me do what I did. I took no pleasure from it, other than knowing it was ultimately an act of kindness.

It's not the same with humans. My empathy levels are much lower. This is on account of the sheer number of us, eight billion or so, and the upper hand we hold over everything around us. We don't need looking after.

I glance quickly to my left. She looks like she was about to say something. When whatever it was crept up on her. I don't think that's right – crept up on her. I don't think she was surprised. I think rather she spent a long time sitting fretfully on the shore of that black, black sea, watching the waves lick higher up the sand, before she simply stood up and waded out into the dark waters.

I reach over the small table between us, the one stained with a thousand cup marks, and hold her wrist. Her skin is cool, but not as cold as I expected. I lift her hand off the armrest and then let it go. I half expect it to hang in mid-air, but it drops back to where it was. There are white fingerprints where I held her.

'Oh, by the way, thanks for dinner last night. I had pizza.'

I lean onto one buttock to pull her credit card out of my back pocket. I hold it up in front of her. She makes no move to take it. I put it on the table.

'I'll just leave it here then, shall I?'

Chapter Four
Then

I see myself sitting in a meeting, eight of us around a long mahogany table. Seven, actually. The eighth is standing up, parading in front of a screen. In my head now I hear, rehear, words such as digitalise, integrity, culture, monetise... I'm not sure if they were on the screen or in his mouth. When he points to something, and he does this frequently, his pink shirt strains between its lower buttons and I'm afforded a tantalising glimpse of his fat, oddly hairless belly. Jason, his name is. He is our new CEO. Everyone despises him. He doesn't fit in, but because he is the new boss it means that none of us fit in anymore. He likes to wear combat trousers on dress-down days. I never mention it.

I glance down at my hand doodling in the notebook. Circles. More circles. Some are more oblong than circular as my hand has grown lazy. The nib has gone round and round so many times none of them look like anything much. Just one big splodge of ink. I turn the page and look at it from the back. The paper has almost worn through, and on the page beneath it the lines have dug messy ruts. I turn over again. And again. I have to turn over nine times before I eventually reach a page without any trace of my handiwork. This, I realise disconsolately, is my total output today. I'm forty-one. I wonder how I've been reduced to this.

My daughter lied this morning. Not to me. She never lies to me. She kids. We kid each other. Like when I told her I'd been to Santa's grotto. How I'd been shopping with my parents when I was about her age and one of his elves appeared in the aisle and said Father Christmas needed my help desperately. I told her I spent the whole afternoon making toys.

'But didn't your parents worry where you were?'

'Oh no. Because Santa stopped time. So, when I appeared in the shop again it was the exact same time as when I left.'

For years she believed that. I almost believe it myself now. But it's a kid, not a lie. They're harmless. The lie she told this morning was to her teacher. She said I was an airline pilot. I was going to protest, but as I opened my mouth something in her face made me stop and I nodded and said, 'Mainly just domestic. The shifts work for us.'

I know why she lied. Because she doesn't understand what I actually do. I've explained it to her more than once, but somehow it doesn't stick. I can't blame her. When I hear it said aloud even I wonder what purpose it serves and why I bother.

'It sounds boring,' she says. 'And you're not boring.'

He's still up there talking. Or, as he'd say, sharing. Or reaching out. Honestly, the words he uses. I've met his wife. She seems lovely. Very kind. Is that why she's never told him his trousers are too tight? But it would be kinder to say something. Surely she must know we all talk behind his back?

I'm not even listening. I'm just sitting back in my chair judging him. Stodgy. He is a stodgy man. He's not tall enough for his considerable bulk, and his face looks like it's been squashed marginally. It's not obvious. At first your eye registers only that something isn't quite correct. Then you look again and realise there is an actual fault in the construction. Unless someone points it out to you, it takes weeks to register that the proportions of width and height are wrong. But once it clicks, it's all you see. That, and the slab of skin that keeps peeking out his shirt. There it is again.

I said there were seven of us around the table. I wonder if they're having their own private monologues as well. They must be. They can't be paying attention to this nonsense. I tune in momentarily.

'...to sync our online output more dynamically with the bricks and mortar side of our business. Revenue targets dictate that...'

I zone out again and glance at the faces around the table. They all appear to be listening. You can never be sure – perhaps in their eyes I'm a study of concentration as well – but they're putting on a fine show if not. I pity them. I begin to feel smug, superior. I'm above all this. I see it for what it is and attribute to it all the regard it merits. Which is disregard. But they've been taken in. Duped. They probably go home and tell their partners about their days, about how they managed to solve this problem or achieve that target, and how pleased their efforts made Jason. I never talk about my work. Fine. That's all I say if I'm asked. It's already wasted enough of my time.

I don't really pity them. I pity myself. I wish I cared as much as they do – or appear to. We all need a purpose in life, and I believe the purpose in life is not happiness but usefulness. These things are not mutually exclusive. How can you be happy if you don't feel useful?

What if I quit my job? I've asked my wife that more times than I can count.

'What would you do instead?'

'I don't know. I'd find something that actually matters. But I never will as long as I'm stuck there.'

She says I'm not a serious man, that she used to like my

dreamy vagueness when we were younger but everyone has to grow up. Even me. She says this, or something like this, a lot. I counter her by explaining that the Aborigines believe we have three brains – one in the gut, one in the heart and one in the head. They believe Western society has lost its way because it has taught itself to ignore the gut and heart, our instincts and emotions, and obey only the logical, the practical. It's not surprising we all suffer from stress and anxiety and depression when we live exclusively in our heads and ignore our passions and deep impulses.

'Okay,' Dolores says, 'I understand that.' She begins walking away and I allow myself to believe I've won the argument. I know there's a catch, but in this brief moment I glimpse what it would feel like. At the door she stops and turns around. 'And in this perfect world of yours I assume we can pay the mortgage with a hunch?'

It was only later, days later, that I realised her response only proved my point; that the brain in our heads always finds ways to talk us out of doing what we feel we need to do.

Where's the fat sales girl today? Not here. She is often not here. Health problems, some suspect, though no one is certain. The rumour is she is sleeping with the boss. I look up at him again. That was definitely a bit of belly button there. How does it work, his sleeping with her? Practically, I mean? His erection can't extend beyond his stomach, and her own protruding roundness must leave them at times just wobbling on top of each other. I think of upturned beetles.

'Something funny?'

He's stopped talking about whatever he was talking about, and is now talking to me.

'No.'

'Oh. I ask only because you are smiling. Do you find this amusing?'

'No, I don't. It doesn't amuse me in the slightest.'

I suddenly realise I've worked here for eleven years. I can remember my first day. I wasn't even enthusiastic then. I sat down at my desk, which was the one furthest from the window, and I've not stood up since.

'Because there is nothing at all funny about our fiscal strategy going forward.' Jason is sweating. His forehead is shining under the light. He uses these words because he's read them in business books and thinks they make him sound articulate. He just sounds like a cunt. 'You of all people should appreciate that. It's your department that will need to pick up the slack at the end of day. We'll need to move forward dynamically to ensure...'

No, I've not stood up since my first day. I've just sat there in the corner, withering away. I stand up now. He stops talking. He looks at me. I feel everyone else looking at me. I feel myself start to blush. I suddenly picture them all dead. Not just dead, but slain, right here and now. I see them slumped over the long desk with puddles of blood seeping out from under their cheeks, or flopped back in their chairs, heads tipped up and lifeless eyes directed at the ceiling. I look at Jason again. He is pinned halfway up that screen of his by a giant spear. I think I threw it. I find I don't mind very much. I've always thought humans were the plague, the infestation eroding and defiling the earth.

'Actually, I think I'm going to be off,' I say.

'Excuse me?'

I hadn't planned to say this and am as shocked as he is. But then, almost indistinguishable at first, I detect a hard kernel of excitement forming in the pit of my stomach. Something unexpected, something with an uncertain outcome, is about to happen, is happening already. An image of my wife's disapproving face pops into my head and I push it away quickly.

I am still holding the pen. I put it down delicately on the scribbled-over page and then close the notepad on it.

'I don't think I can,' I say.

'What?'

'Excuse you. I don't think I can anymore.' That kernel is a stone now. I am beginning to feel almost giddy. 'You were talking about moving forward dynamically. I agree. And now I'm going to move forward dynamically to the door.'

They say it's like floating. I'd not describe it that way. I feel painfully self-conscious as I walk down the length of the room, listening to my brogues squeaking on the floorboards. I am aware of the movement of all my limbs and have to consciously swing them in a way that I hope seems natural. Someone calls my name. There is a question mark after it. I keep going. I can't wait to tell Grace. She'll be so proud.

At the door I stop.

'So, just to be clear, I've quit. I'm going to be a pilot.'

Chapter Five
Now

What I find astonishing is that Flo lived here in this flat with her husband for fifty-eight years. Before he died a little more than twelve years ago. I think that's worth repeating. She lived here in this flat with her husband for fifty-eight years. The mind boggles. That is some achievement. I can't decide if I envy or pity her. A bit of both. For never leaving, and for never needing to. Dolores and I would have driven each other crazy. I've not said much about Dolores yet. I suppose that says a lot in itself. I will though.

'I still speak to him,' Flo told me once, 'him and the plants. But it isn't the same. I have to imagine what he says back to me and I know I'm probably wrong half the time. He never stopped surprising me. Even at the end. Not in a dramatic way. But sometimes he'd say something, and I'd stare at him and think, *Who is this man?*'

She says it was just blind luck. Her successful marriage.

'There but for the grace of God,' she said. Only old people say that. She told me that she and her sister both fell pregnant in their middle teens. They lived further up the coast, in the grander part of an even smaller town. Their father was, what was he, I forget, but he was respected somehow. The vicar used to come for tea. No family, least of all theirs, wanted a scandal like that. It would have sullied the name for generations. It wouldn't have. People forget. People have their own scandals. But that's what they thought then.

'I'd only known Len for about six months when I realised I was late.' Flo gave me a sly look to make sure I understood. 'My sister was in the same boat. I think we even met them, Len and Jack, at the same dance. We did everything together then, you see, my sister and I. We'd shared a room since we were little. I'd drawn a chalk line down the middle of it and she wasn't allowed to cross it or there'd be a mighty fuss. But we were best friends, too. And then this happened. And there was such a stigma about it in those days. I remember we were terrified to tell our parents. But they were very matter of fact. Very practical about it. There was never any discussion. We were both married within a month. It didn't matter a jot that they were complete strangers. Not to me, at least. But then I was the lucky one. Len was a good man, bless his soul. He never hurt me. He always worked hard. He was always kind. But Jack. Well.'

Flo shook her head and for a long time didn't say anything else. I said about old people leaking from the outside corners of their eyes. That's when I noticed it. She was facing the window and I saw the wet silver trail in a claw of her crow's feet. As I watched she removed her glasses and dabbed her eyes with a tissue that had been folded beneath the sleeve of her cardigan.

'He was horrible,' she continued. 'Such a nasty piece of work from the word go. I told Margaret to leave him, but how could she? Where would she go? It was different then. He was awful to her. And then, to cap it all off, he fell off a ladder barely a year later and was paralysed. So, she had to look after him and the baby. And that was her life. He was only meant to live for about five years, after the accident, so we kept waiting. But the blasted man didn't die. He outlived her and the child in the end. Out of stubbornness. He just wore them down. It was such a shame to watch. Such a waste of a life. She was always so much brighter than me, and prettier. She could have done anything. Who knows what she'd have made of herself today, with the opportunities we have.

'I think sometimes my own life has been wasted on me. She'd have made far more of it. But there you are. I've been happy. Len was a good man.'

I've seen pictures of them. She was a bit of a stunner in her heyday. Even at the end, in fact, when she smiled in a certain way, the beauty she once was reappeared. Not in the same way of course. The wrinkles don't vanish. The blotches. But you could see the structure, the expression, the way the features moved to let the light out. It was an internal smile. I imagine Len must have felt like a million dollars when she smiled at him like that.

Where's the boy? That's what I want to know. They have a son. I know everything there is to know about him. She's made sure of that. He is a high achiever. A self-starter. A go-getter. But he's not let it go to his head, that's the good thing. He has a wonderful family whom he loves and respects. And he plays sport to a high level. He could have been a contender. But he was too high-minded. More worthy things to focus on. He supports charities. He builds churches in remote regions. He loves animals and children and the underprivileged. He's cured cancer and he's working on world peace. Where would we be without him? Derek. That's his name. Flo is incredibly proud of him. And with good reason, if even half of what she says is true. I don't believe it is. I've seen a picture of him. Make that plural.

Pictures. He has no chin. None at all. His face just seems to fall away below his lip and then suddenly there is his neck. He has tiny eyes too. Little black pellets that look like they should be peering out of a rabbit's face. I can't criticise his hair though. He has fine hair. A big thick silver mop. It's very distinguished. Maybe that's how he managed to do everything he's done. He just shook his fabulous mane in their faces. Swoon. Even the men. I have no hair. Almost none. Not on my head anyway. It seemed to all drop out at once during a single fraught night a few years ago. I woke up the next morning and lifted my head off the pillow, but my hair remained where it was. I'd only just moved in here. It was really quite alarming. A few resolute strands remain. But they have slid off my scalp and set up residence on and in my ears. I can feel them if I hover a finger just above the skin. It tickles.

So where is he? Why is this on me? This – she – is becoming an imposition. It's not my job. To do anything about her. She's not my responsibility. No one even knows we're friends. I live next door. So what? People don't know their neighbours anymore. And Christ knows who lives downstairs. I think it's a holiday home of some sort. I never see anyone. I certainly never see the same person twice. Don't I have my own issues?

I glance at her now. What's left of her. I should have called someone immediately. No one deserves this. I could call someone now. It's not too late. I feel in my back pocket. There is something hard in there. I take it out. It's her credit card again. How did it get back in there? I've been using it for days. Why have I? I have my own money. I try to explain my actions in my head. I sound guilty even to myself. I lean back in my chair. Not my chair. Len's chair. I put my feet up on the windowsill. She doesn't like me doing this. I'm taking liberties now. But who can stop me? No one can.

The phone is ringing. Now I notice it I realise that it's rung before. It's so loud and intrusive. It sounds almost vulgar in this deathly silence.

'Well? It won't be for me.'

A button clicks and someone starts speaking. A man's voice. I've never heard it before, but I know immediately who it is.

'Doris? Are you there? Pick up if you are. I've been calling all day.' I can hear him breathing into the mouthpiece. 'He means you,' I mouth silently. She says nothing. 'A lot's happened this end.' This end. Jesus. Let's touch base. 'I'll come see you.'

My first reaction is one of panic. Does he mean now? Is he on the stairwell this instant? Does he have a key? I wonder who would be more shocked. I look quickly out of the window at the road. There are no cars either pulling up or parked. But he may be just around the corner. I scan the room for signs of me. If I leave now, what would I leave behind? But no. He doesn't mean now. He means whenever. He means sometime in the future. When it is convenient. I sit back down in Len's chair and sip my cold tea. I've always believed it is polite to leave a little in the cup. It suggests to the host you are sated. That they have served you sufficiently, met all your needs. I don't know where I learned that. Someone must have told me once.

Good. He will find her. I won't be involved. No, I'll say, I didn't smell anything. But I've got no sense of smell. My apologetic face. Palms turned upwards. The door closing. Footsteps on the stairs. Sirens departing. And this will all be over.

Chapter Six
Then

My dog is a pain in the arse. I love him, but he is a real pain the arse. He is nearly blind and pretends when it's convenient to be nearly deaf too. But I know he hears me when I call him. He stops what he is doing. He freezes on the spot with his ears pricked. He turns his head slowly and looks in my general direction but never right at me. And then, as if deciding that it's nothing important, that I'm nothing important, he dismisses me and trots the other way. No amount of calling will stop him then.

If this sounds like thinly veiled admiration that's because it is. No man is his master. He does just whatever the fuck he wants. And he gets away with it. That is the nub of it. I might be the one to feed him, to care for him, to provide a home for him. I might have bought him that expensive basket which he never sleeps in – too proud – and all those toys he never plays with. But none of this means anything. He will still do just whatever the fuck he wants.

He's watching me now. While he squats low over his hind legs in that most unbecoming of poses. I've heard people say that dogs look at their owners while shitting because that's when they are most vulnerable, and they seek our reassurance. Maybe that's true for some dogs. Not him. I know his face. He's challenging me to judge him. I'm a dog. This is what we do. That's what his face is saying. If he could raise an eyebrow I'm sure he would. Sure, he can see me now. Nothing wrong with his sight now. When he's finished he turns around and gives his handiwork a quick sniff. Suitably repellent. Then he trots off. Not a care in the world. I am watching him go. The act isn't over. I'm waiting for the final gesture. The look of disdain he always throws over his shoulder at me. There. There it is. Pick that up, his look says.

His excrement is hot through the thin bag. Welcome on cold days, but it is spring and the sun is nearly out. I should be at work right now. It is four days since my career came to an unanticipated end. The weekend has been jammed in the middle so it has really only been two days. No time to sink in yet, and standing in the middle of a field at 10.15 on a Tuesday morning is still novel to me, like it isn't even happening yet.

'I should be doing geography right now.'

'I should be at work.'

Grace and I exchange conspiratorial glances. Her eyes twinkle. In the back of the car is a bag with her school uniform and my suit. We left the house wearing them, waving goodbye to Dolores – Mummy – as we reversed out the drive. I drove straight past her school though. I didn't even slow down.

'Daddy!' She had no idea.

'It's under control,' I said.

We changed in the McDonald's toilets, had one of their plastic breakfasts, something I'd never normally do, and then when it was safe, when we knew Dolores – Mummy – had gone, we went back to pick up Reggie. We often walk through these farmer's fields at weekends, following the narrow uneven paths that cut straight lines through the crops. It is different now. The world seems quieter.

'What's the capital of France?' I ask.

'Paris.'

'Spot on. Geography lesson over.'

Reggie has gone. Something has caught his nose and he's vanished into the fields somewhere. Sometimes if there is no wind you can follow him by watching the grass move, but not today. A strong breeze swirls around us, making all the stems shiver and lean one way then the other.

'Reggie!' I call. But the wind blows my voice back down my throat. Reggie wouldn't listen to me anyway. I've never learnt to whistle properly, that two-fingered whistle that makes everyone around look and wish they could do it too. We stop, Grace and I, and scan around us like two tower guards facing in opposite directions.

'There!' she says, after a few minutes.

Reggie's head always pops up somewhere completely different from where we expect it to. Even from this distance we can see him looking at us with a huge grin on his face. As I said, he knows. We call him again. He doesn't move. If Grace wasn't here I'd swear.

'Come on!' I shout.

He ducks down into the stalks again and is gone.

Dogs do grin. They don't just have one face. If you know your dog you'll get to recognise all their different expressions. Not as many as humans, but I prefer them anyway. They're less complicated. Sometimes with humans their expressions don't match what they're feeling. That never happens with dogs. You know exactly what they're feeling when they look at you. Reggie really smiles at me. It makes me smile. Go on then, you beast. He'd bound away. A pheasant would burst out of the long grass.

I put my arm around Grace. She is the perfect height.

'This is the life, isn't it?'

'You're naughty.'

'Only in the conventional way. The classroom isn't the only place you can learn. I don't even think it's the best place.'

'You know where I sit in the class, right at the back by the wall?' I say I do. 'It's annoying because it's really hot in the summer and really cold in the winter. I sat there last year, too. It's not fair. I asked Miss if...'

She's my daughter and I love her, but it's impossible to listen to her all the time. I'd never do anything else. I don't know where she gets all her words from. At the start I used to try to engage every time she spoke. No matter how pointless it seemed. The most important thing you can give your children is attention. I'd read that somewhere, and was determined to follow through. I lasted perhaps a year. Then it just became exhausting. And often I don't actually need to listen. She'll ask a question and before I have time to process her query she's answered it herself or withdrawn it.

'Actually, don't worry. It doesn't matter.'

Instead, I like to watch her. She is a fascinating mover. She speaks with her hands. Like her mother. That's why she is so clumsy. Broken plates, spilled drinks, grazed knuckles. 'Oh, guess what?' Crash. Over goes a bowl. Her mother isn't clumsy though. She might have been at this age, at nine, but she was already far too deliberate when I met her to do anything accidentally, without suitable consideration and planning.

Grace's mouth is moving. Her hands are flying all around her. Did she accidentally thump me in the ribs a few minutes ago, or was that another day? I prod around my abdomen feeling for a bruise. I should try to listen more though. I know we've got all the time in the world, and she will never stop talking to me, but children say remarkable things sometimes. Without meaning to. Things that cut through the white noise and stick in your mind so vividly that years later you remember them exactly. You remember where you were. The weather. The way they made you feel and how all the adults stopped talking.

'Do you even still like Mummy?' That was one of those things.

I lay the blanket out beside the path and we settle down. It isn't really warm enough for a picnic. There is a chill. The sun keeps coming and going and we keep looking up to see how big the cloud is and how far away the next patch of blue sky is.

'Are you really going to become a pilot?'

I told her about my job the same day, but made her promise not to tell her mother yet. She was so excited. Partly because of what I'd done and partly because it was another secret between us. She had got out of bed and formally shaken my hand. Good luck, today is the first day of the rest of your life. I don't know where she heard that, but it made me feel good. Like I could walk on water.

'I could become anything I want now,' I said.

'Not anything. You're a bit old.'

I lie back on the path with my hands under my head. The light on the other side of my eyelids goes light and dark, light and dark as the clouds fly across the sky. I hear a train rattle past us. Reggie barks at it and I hear Grace get up and go running after him. A darker shadow falls over me and I open my eyes. A woman is standing there. She has six dogs on six different leads. They are all sitting patiently, waiting for a signal from their pack leader.

'I'd keep him on a lead here, if I were you. We've lost a few to the tracks.'

I say thanks and stand up, looking across the field for Grace and the beast. The woman is still here. She's not looking across the fields. She's looking at me. I can see her out of the corner of my eye. I'm beginning to feel uneasy. Because she's here, but mainly because I can't see Grace. I don't want to show this woman I'm uneasy though. I'm beginning to really dislike her. What if I picked up a rock and hit her on the head with it? I wouldn't do that. Not with the six dogs there. I smile at her.

'They're fine,' I say, then lie back down and close my eyes again. I know when she finally walks on because she takes her shadow with her and my eyelids go suddenly warm.

The unease is still there. It's a little more than unease. It's nothing to do with Grace or the beast. I said they were fine and I believe it. No, the unease is about myself; my own predicament. I realise this quite suddenly and with a sense of let-down, like when you're young and you think you can run fast and then find out there are many children who can run faster. Shit. I'm beginning to think I might have fucked up. I'm going to move forward dynamically to the door. I felt like a king when I said that. But now what? I am unemployed. I have no prospect of employment. It's too late to start afresh. You're a bit old. She was right. I could end up in a supermarket. Or a petrol station. Dolores wouldn't hang around to watch that. The unease is bordering on panic now. I can feel my heart racing. It seems they were right, all those people who thought – and think – she is too good for me. I am one of them. I am sure there are times when she regrets it. I think men can tell if their woman wants them. I know they can tell if they don't. She was the prettiest girl in the school. Everyone thought so. Girls go from children to women over the summer. They leave for the holidays as one thing and return as something else. Male teachers are suddenly uncomfortable around them. Wary. They notice the change. But not boys. Boys stay children for ages. Their bodies outgrow their brains. They are too strong and long-limbed for the games they still play. Dolores was always so far ahead of me. Ahead of everyone. I'm actually older than her by a few months, but it's never felt that way. I didn't expect her to say yes when I asked her out. We were sixteen. She didn't say yes as such. She said sure. Why not. It wasn't a no. No one could believe it.

'But what did she actually say?'

'She's just taking the piss.'

She didn't say yes when I asked her to marry me, either. She really did say no then. The first time. A year later, when I asked again, she said fine. That also surprised me. That was twelve years ago, twelve blissful years of holy matrimony. She's now the prettiest woman. I recognise this on an intellectual level. People see us together and assume I must be rich. No, she's the one who is rich, I want to say. She is the one who has the good job and goes on overseas business trips. Often with Joe. I've met Joe. They look good together. Well-matched. He is her boss, but not her superior. He has a dimple on his chin. He's not even English. He has an accent. She's told me about it. I wonder about them sometimes. No, I'm not rich. I don't know if she is. We don't share accounts. The house, which is too big for us, is in her name.

'Do you even still like Mummy?'

She'll be off now. She won't stand for this. I have a vision of my future self. Dishevelled and depressed in a single room in a deprived part of town. Getting up every morning, putting on my blue overalls and going to the petrol station. Walking home with a brown paper bag, taking secret swigs. Not secret. I won't even care who watches. But it won't be alcohol that gets me. I don't even like alcohol. I know what it will be. I will text him. I don't smoke around Grace. That's my rule. I wait until after bedtime. But now I'm at home all day... Yes, I will text him. The start of the descent. I'm not going to become a pilot. What a stupid idiot you are. You can't even see properly. Pump number six? That's forty-two pounds, please, sir. And just because I thought I was too good for that boardroom. I want to sit back down quietly. When I stood up. I want to go back and sit back down in my chair and think up a suitable response to the question of moving forward dynamically. I could be a team player if I tried. Fuck's sake. What now? Aborigines. Three brains. What a load of shit. I'm lying still, the sun is still coming and going, but inside I feel like a shark thrashing about on a deck.

'Daddy?'

I nearly jump out of my skin. Grace is standing there with Reggie.

'We were spying on you. You didn't hear us, did you?'

'Not a sound.'

We're walking back now. We've agreed to get up before dawn one morning and come back here. We think we might see deer. Or a fox. It will never happen. The deer might be here. And the fox. But we'll never return.

'What did that woman want?' Grace asks.

'Which woman?'

'The one with all the dogs?'

'Oh. Nothing. She was being a busybody. Telling us to watch out for the train tracks.' I roll my eyes at Grace and she rolls hers back at me. 'We play by our own rules,' I say to her, and she puts her fist out and we knock knuckles lightly. I'm a superhero when I'm with her.

Chapter Seven

Now

I'm sitting in Len's chair again. Back at the scene of the crime. Just joking. What crime? It's been two weeks. I've still not called anyone. There is absolutely no way I can now. It seems I'm really doing this. I can't claim any longer to be a passive participant. I am without doubt playing an active role. Not doing something is the same as doing something else. Not making a decision is the same as making a different decision. I've started watering the plants – her plants – as part of my daily routine. It's a sort of homage. I do it in the evenings, after taking delivery of my food order. Yes. That's another thing that has become habitual. I have the same toppings every time.

What else? I've set up a few direct debits to pay her essential bills – council tax, utilities – and I even put some of my rubbish in her bins. I don't think this last bit is necessary. I do it anyway.

And I've started telling her things. These last few days. About before I got here. And how I ended up here. How I went from a job, a wife, a daughter, a home, to this. It's quite a fall from grace. No offence, Flo. It doesn't take as much as you'd think. You'd imagine that there must be a whole series of calamities that smash everything up. Because we think, most of us do, I certainly did, we think our foundations are so strong. We imagine all the important things in our lives that make our lives what they are to be permanent structures. Great big cement pillars in the ground. They're not. You can turn left instead of right and everything falls apart.

'It happened so fast,' I tell Flo. 'Did it for you?'

She doesn't answer. She just sits there rotting in her chair. Starting to stick to it. She is beginning to look a state. She had started decomposing even before she died, but the process has really taken a grip of her now. What she's becoming is almost indecent. It's quite marvellous in its own way, even fascinating, but it's not for the squeamish. When I have the stomach for it I'll describe what I see, and what happens when I prod her skin. But apart from the detached curiosity, I do feel terrible for her. She took such pride in her appearance. Even at her age. I'm so glad she can't see herself. She would be distraught.

'Don't come in,' she'd shout through the door. 'I'm not decent.'

No, she's not. A few days ago I went around her flat laying the mirrors down. Just in case.

Often we won't talk at all though. I'll just sit beside her, breathing through my mouth, looking at the sea and wondering how it changes colour so completely from one day to the next. The thing is, I didn't plan any of this. I really didn't. Yet, oddly, it feels natural. Almost like a continuation of what was before. I know that's not how it will be portrayed when the newspapers get hold of this story, as surely they must. What will I be made into? A macabre monster. The Beast of the Beachfront. The Seaside Savage. They do love the outlandish. I shudder at the prospect. People reading it. My former workmates. He was always a little odd. He kept himself to himself. There was just something about him. But I never expected this. And to think I spent all those years sitting right next to him.

I realise something now; humiliation is not about the act, it's about who sees the act. It needs an audience to exist. What can we possibly do alone to leave ourselves humiliated? I think nothing. So humiliation is about ego, not conscience.

I wonder if the news will reach across the Channel, to where Grace has been taken? I hope they don't track her down. I'd hate to think of cameras on her lawn, photos of her shielding her eyes as she's shepherded to the car before school. I'm exaggerating. It's hardly that big a story. Front page in the local paper, perhaps page five in a few nationals. Forgotten the next day. That's all this is.

Grace will find out though. I can't help that. I'm sorry, little friend. Don't hate me. Or rather, don't hate me more than you do already. She'd deny it. I know she would. But I can tell from her letters. I'm fine. We're fine. Hope you're fine. Anyone could've written them. There is nothing of her in there. It reads like a chore. It's not her fault. It's her mother's doing. It's her repugnant influence. Poor Grace only hears one side of the story. But she should know me better than that. Whatever she is getting told I am, she must know I'm not. I thought we had an unbreakable bond. Children are so cruel. So carelessly cruel.

'Even yours, Flo. No–' I raise a finger at her. 'Don't argue. You know it's true. Even yours.'

I'm thinking about a day just like today. I was sitting right here. On Len's chair. He'll be here at eleven, she said. I must come around, she said. I'd finally get to meet him, she said. It was nearly noon and we were still waiting. She was trying to appear nonchalant but I could tell that she was pressing something down. It was tiring her out and making her a little tetchy to be honest.

'Please,' she snapped at me.

I took my feet off the windowsill.

There were biscuits behind us. A nice selection. With cream and chocolate and bits of dried fruit. I'd not eaten yet. I was expecting to be back in my own flat by now. I kept thinking of the biscuits on the plate and licking my lips.

'He's a bright boy. Always has been. I don't know where he got it from because Len and me were never up to much. He works in finance, you know.' I did know. 'He was in America for a while. And Hong Kong. He's so busy. We're very proud of him.' Who's we? Don't include me in this. 'And he's got a wonderful family. I think you'll really like him.'

'When he gets here.'

'Yes. When he gets here.'

Flo was jabbering. Filling up the time. Cars passed beneath the window but none of them stopped. I looked out at the ocean. There was a shipwreck somewhere out there. At low tide you could see it. People drowned. The rescue operation was launched from this very beach. I wondered if she and Len had watched the drama unfold from this spot.

'Feet,' Flo said again.

'Sorry.'

Eventually a car pulled up outside and we both sat forward. All four doors opened and a family – father, mother, two children – climbed out onto the pavement. But it was the wrong family. They crossed the road and disappeared down the steps onto the beach. We watched the empty sand until they emerged from under the angle of the promenade and unpacked their deckchairs and towels.

'He's so busy,' Flo said again, almost to herself.

I got up and reboiled the kettle. I put a tea towel over the biscuits. I didn't eat one. I looked at the tray beside them, with her nice cups all prepared with teaspoons in them. With a little jug of milk and a matching bowl of sugar. It was her best set. She'd laid it all out even before I got there. The milk was probably going off already. I looked at the back of her head and suddenly felt awful for her.

'That's a good idea,' she said without turning around. 'Get everything ready now because I'm sure he'll be in a rush. He's so busy.'

I put her cup and my cup on the little table between us and sat back down. The parents on the beach had settled deep into their deckchairs. The two children were the black dots far out in the water. There wasn't a single moment when I realised he wasn't coming. But I knew by then. I didn't want to be there anymore. I couldn't stand to see it. What I said about humiliation. I picked up our cups again and returned them to the counter. I put the milk in the fridge. Flo was as still then as she is now. I closed the door quietly behind me and returned to my own flat.

So I'm not worried about his phone call now. It was days ago. I've hardly given it a second thought. He said he was coming to visit. He's said that before. I lean over in Len's chair to face Flo. The smell makes me want to cough but I suppress it. Out of politeness.

'Life is so unfair,' I say. 'Don't you think?'

Months ago, sitting just where she is now, Flo told me how she'd learned not to take things personally, to accept that life doesn't know who we are or what we've done and is nothing more than a series of random actions. She didn't say random. She said arbitrary. It suited her mouth even less than random would have. She said life was arbitrary and good things happen to bad people and bad things happen to good people. She was talking about Margaret and Jack. I think she was.

'You know that's a load of shit, don't you, Flo. How can you not take things personally? Surely that's the only way to take them? It makes me angry. I want to lash out. To break things. Don't you ever feel like that? You must. I saw your face the other day, when he phoned. That flicker of hope in your eye. Don't worry if you don't. I'll feel it for you. On your behalf.'

Chapter Eight
Then

I am like Pavlov's dog. You know the one whose mouth started drooling for food whenever he rang the bell? It proved our bodies react to the thought of something, not just the thing itself. I am driving through the centre of town. I'd have gone another way if there was another way to go, but there isn't. There are cars everywhere. The driver in front of me is always the slowest on the road. Until I change lanes and the new slowest driver is in front of me. The lights are red each time. They must be doing work on the signalling system because they are red for me much longer than for anyone else.

I texted my man last night. After our day in the fields. All the old language came back immediately. I was that person again. *Cheese. Big bags.* The stupid way of spelling things. *Ye.* It had been a long time, a good few years. But I was that person again. I realised he was always in me. Not the addict. But the addicted. The moment the idea had come back into my head I was itching for it. Ants in my pants.

'What's wrong with you? Sit still, will you?'

I kept checking my phone all evening. He didn't have anything when I first texted him. He was getting 'sum' later. So vague. Later? When the fuck is later? Half an hour? Another life? But you can't press. *Cool,* I said, *text wen u get sum.* A part of me died writing that. And sending it. A middle-aged man. Respectable. Until recently, employed. A father. A husband. But also, a part of me came alive. I kept checking my phone. I turned it off and on to make sure it was working. I asked Dolores to text me to make sure I had a signal even though I knew I did. It wasn't until 11.39pm that he texted back. *Got sum, mate.* I tried to justify going out then, at that hour. But I couldn't do it. You've got to have some boundaries. I said I'd be round in the morning.

How slow did Grace walk? I've never noticed this before. But walking from the car to the school was like crossing the Gobi.

'Come on, you'll be late.' Trying to keep the edge out of my voice. My face strained but trying to seem relaxed. And then her teacher accosting me at the door.

'We're teaching aviation. Orville and Wilbur Wright. Perhaps you'd like to come in and talk to the class?'

I stared, nonplussed. What was she talking about?

'With you being a pilot and everything.'

It didn't take as long walking back to the car. Nowhere near. I didn't run. But I went nearly as fast. Everything else was in place. The papers, the tobacco, a new lighter. You never escape the feeling of being judged, buying it all. It was safely tucked away in the door panel. All I needed now was the little bank bag. And that was only thirty minutes away.

The car in front stops to let a group of children cross. All holding hands in a long chain. I breathe deeply. I use the break to pick up my phone. *On way now,* I text. No reply. I drive on. To the outskirts of town. The traffic is thinner here. Past the warehouse. Still no reply. But then my message didn't need a reply. It was a statement of fact. I turn left and pick up speed. Farmland and hills either side now. How many times have I driven this road? With just this impatience. Dolores used to join in. Before Grace. And when Grace was young. We used to have great sex then. Not so much now. The sex or the joining in. Through another small town. More of a village than a town. Barely in it then I'm out the other side. Still no reply. Just confirmation. That's all I'm looking for. Until then there is always a doubt. It's not like buying milk. Anything could happen. These people aren't the most reliable. I check my phone again. *C u soon.* Boom. There it is!

Ten minutes later I'm pulling up on the kerb. I've already texted my arrival. *Here mate.* I did that when I turned the last corner. Not a moment to waste. I sit and wait.

These are the things I know: I am shamed. I feel shame. To be here. In this area. It's basically a slum. It's not my world. If I got mugged here, or stabbed, how would I explain it? It's not the area though. I'm not a snob. That's one thing I'm not. It's what I'm doing here. At 9.36 on a Wednesday morning. I can't lie. It represents failure. You can talk about addictive personalities and so on. That's just excuses. It doesn't take away personal responsibility. I made every single decision that was required to get me here, to this spot. It wasn't one decision. One moment of weakness. There were many. But I also know I'm not leaving and that right now I wouldn't want to be anywhere else in the world. I'm almost shaking with anticipation. And that part of me loves the juxtaposition of being who I am, coming from the world I do, into this one.

I check my phone. *Come to the gate.* That's not usual. He's never asked that before. Normally he just slides in the passenger side. I get out and walk up the path that leads between the houses. Lots of windows all overlooking me. I don't care.

Everyone around here knows what's going on. I stop at the gate. It's wooden. It has broken panels and rot. I think if I tried to open it, it would fall off its hinges. A moment later the back door opens and he walks towards me. Immediately I feel better. He is wearing a tracksuit. Or *the* tracksuit. It's the same one he always wears. It has stretched around the knees. I notice he has a tag around his ankle. Ah. That explains the gate. But he has a baby face. He is smiling. He doesn't look like what he is. We shake hands. I give him the money. He gives me the bag. I'm walking back down the path. I feel so much lighter already. Like I've already started smoking it. Pavlov's dog. Woof, woof.

Chapter Nine
Now

I took Flo out once. For her birthday. It was her eightieth. She said it was her eightieth but I suspect there were a few more miles on the clock. I hadn't planned to. It just happened. It seems a lot of things just happen to me, without my say-so.

I had been down to the beach for my early morning swim. How long was I under that time? Not long I don't think. My heart wasn't in it. I remember looking up at the chicks on the way back. They were still there, the two of them, on the chimney. One of them walked to the edge and I got my first proper look at him. A seagull. Scruffy. That's what I thought. The short feathers on the back of his neck were sticking up. He was nearly full size but grey all over. He looked unsure of himself. The way he stood there. Looking down the tiles of the roof. Looking out to sea. Up at the sky. Could he fly then? Could he even comprehend flying? I think he could sense he had big things ahead of him. Maybe he was worried they would come before he was ready. Just above him and to the side, one of his parents – I'm making an assumption here – was standing straight-backed, beak up, watching for threats. Every so often it looked down at me. *Squawk. Squawk.* It was a warning. The whole scene pleased me immeasurably. They're not so different from us. I know we like to think we're special, but we're not so special. Their instincts overlap our own. We're all animals at heart.

When I opened the door I saw Flo, as before, standing above the plant pots with her watering can. She wasn't pouring. She only started pouring when she looked up and saw me.

'Happy birthday,' I said. 'I thought you'd be gone by now.'

The Great White Hope, that's what I call Derek, was taking her out. She had bought a new frock specially. She had tried it on for me the previous day. I said that blue suited her. I didn't say it brought out her veins.

'Len always said that.' She was pleased. The dress had cost a little bit more than she wanted to pay but she was very glad it fitted as well as it did. 'I needed a new one. I think it's quite a grand restaurant he's taking me to,' she'd said. 'But you must pop around before we go and say hello. You can finally meet him.'

I walked up the stairs towards her. She'd not answered me. When I'd wished her happy birthday. She was still pouring.

'Flo?' I asked.

She looked up. It's hard to tell with old people, I mean really old people, if they're crying or if their eyes are just wet.

'What time is your lunch?'

She didn't say anything. We just stood there for a few moments. My wet feet were leaving footprints. She was still pouring. The pots were leaking at the bottom. Muddy streams were trickling out on to the carpet.

'Is he still coming?'

'He's been called away,' she said.

I lifted an arm towards her. It got halfway and then fell back again. It felt awkward. That wasn't really me. I'm not a tactile person.

'It must be very important,' I said. I walked past her to my

44

own door. She had stopped pouring now. Her arms were hanging limp by her sides. The empty can was rocking on the carpet and she was still just standing there in front of the plants with her back to me.

'We can go out, if you like?'

'You don't want to do that.'

'It won't be the same. Nowhere grand. But we can have a bite somewhere?'

'You don't want to waste your time.'

'It would be my pleasure.' I was only being polite but when I said it I realised it was true.

That's the most important bit. That I took her out on her birthday. The rest doesn't matter. It doesn't matter that we only went to one of those silent tearooms with frilly tablecloths and the thin tinkle of spoons on saucers. No one ever seems to be in these places. How do they make any money? I don't think they do. I imagine the owner to be a widow with a military pension and a nest egg who wants the company more than the income.

I even gave Flo a present. I can't claim to have gone out to buy it. It was a book that had been left in the flat by the previous owner. It was in good condition though. I'd found it at the back of a shelf in one of the cupboards months ago. Since then it had just sat on the end of the bed. It was a book about seabirds. I thought it was appropriate. For us. Considering the hours we spent in front of the window.

She opened it to a random page. 'Nicknamed the sea-parrot or clown of the sea, the puffin spends most of its life at sea, resting on the waves when not swimming. Their range spans the eastern coast of Canada and the United States to the western coast of Europe.' She stopped talking but continued reading. 'Did you know they flap their wings four hundred times a minute? And can dive sixty metres? Well I never.' She put the book down and took her glasses off. 'You're a good boy.'

A good boy, she said. A good boy indeed. If she could've seen into my head. I was thinking of the Great White Hope. Of Derek. I was wondering where he was at that exact moment. Probably sat in his office with his trousers around his ankles and his secretary on her knees. I think if she'd looked properly at my face she'd have realised I was mulling over something quite unpleasant. 'You'll finally get to meet him,' she said. I'd like to have met him just then. At that precise moment. I looked around for something solid that I would have used.

Chapter Ten
Then

Dolores is talking to me now. I've not said much about her. Well here she is. Sitting on the couch barely two yards away. She is just back from work. She is wearing a pencil skirt and sheer blouse. The blouse is untucked. It just hangs off of her. How am I meant to concentrate? We used to have sex all the time. Not just sex. We used to fuck. I see us in a tent. There are shadows of people moving all around us. She is beneath me and sweating. My sweat is dripping onto her. We are staring at each other. And utterly silent. I see us in the front room. It is night. A lamp is on behind us. She is pressed against the large window. Naked. Her arse is pushing back to meet me. We are in the car. I'm driving and she is in my lap. We're in a pool. Another couple is there too. They don't know.

This stuff all happened. I look at her now. I imagine her with her skirt hiked up around her waist. Her underwear either yanked down or to the side. I imagine her small but perfectly formed breasts jiggling. My hand reaches round and squeezes one, pushing her cleavage up into the gap between her top buttons.

I can't help myself. I can't help wanting her like this. I wish I didn't. It would be so much easier. But she's sexy as fuck. I've always thought so. Lascivious. The word pops up out of nowhere like an unsolicited erection. And I'm not the only one. I see men in the street. The way they look at her. I'm right there but it's like I don't exist. I don't blame them. They can't help themselves. Just like I can't. I imagine them saving her up for a quiet time. When they're alone. I look over my shoulder after we've passed them and they're doing the same thing. Storing. A final look. I can't tell you what it is about her. She's not even beautiful. But some people are beautiful and forgettable. Dolores is not forgettable. Some people even think she's very nearly ugly – that's the part Grace has inherited; it breaks my heart – but even they remember her. Maybe it's her red hair. It's so red it's almost orange. You'd assume it was dyed but it's not. And she's a true redhead. She doesn't trim. I love that. I could dive in there for hours. She's a mottled mess when she's wet enough. All the strands sticking together. Maybe it's her blue eyes they remember. In a school essay Grace said they were as blue as the bluest crystal in the cave. I can't improve on that.

She is still talking. I keep setting and resetting my listening face. If I was really listening I wouldn't have to think about it. She's talking about work. She looks so serious. When did she get so serious? I wish she'd laugh more. Blah-blah-blah, she is saying. Blah-blah-blah Joe. Blah-blah-blah Joe.

It's not my fault. I'm a little stoned. I've been to see my friend again. And again. I've had six today. Or seven. I had to pick Grace up in my sunglasses. She tried to take them off of me but I wouldn't let her. We went for ice cream instead.

'You can't eat all of that, Daddy?'

'Just you watch me.'

It's always like this. I wish it wasn't. I wish I was a responsible adult. It's just as well I don't drink. The first time I went back there, to the broken gate that is still broken, I felt the full force of it again. It had been months after all. I remember driving home incredibly slowly but feeling it was as fast as I could go. There was a line of cars. I had to pull over. I toppled sideways onto the passenger seat and remained there for an hour or so. The blood had all drained out of my head and gathered in my limbs. The weight of them. I couldn't lift them. But after that first one the same thing happened as always happened. I got used to it again. I have a tolerance for it. After so many years. So I need to keep smoking. It might actually be eight so far today. My record is sixty-two for a weekend. I'm not proud. If I sound proud, I'm not. I wish I could stop. I wish I'd never started. I wonder who I'd be now?

Dolores hasn't noticed. Or she's not said if she has. She wants to go to Dubai. That's what I've gathered so far. She's not come out and said it yet, but that's what this is leading up to. She's taking the scenic route there. All the while I'm nodding. I've knotted my eyebrows. My listening face. How should I act when she does finally come out with it? What attitude will give me the greatest chance with her later on tonight? Disappointed but understanding. Oh dear. Really? Must you go? No, you go. It's important to you. That means it's important to me. The supportive husband. I've read about him in magazines. He's got it all figured out.

'It's a fantastic opportunity,' she says. 'Joe thinks...'

She leans forward and her blouse falls opens a little. I can't help looking. Maybe she sees me ogling her. Because that's what I'm doing. I won't sugar-coat it. I'm pawing her with my eyes while still wearing this professional, modern-man mask. It's quite a trick. She leans back again and my fun is over. I glance down at her thighs. The way she's sitting side-on has hitched her skirt up. Women's legs beneath black nylon. I can feel my body start to tingle. It's eight today. I'm sure now. It always has this effect on me. I imagine the men in her office standing in the doorway and staring where I'm staring.

'It sounds very promising,' I say. She'd stopped talking. I don't think there was too much dead air before I realised. 'You can't really say no.'

But she can say no. I've heard her say no.

She nods slowly at me. She purses her lips and shrugs. It can't be helped, her manner says. Like she's just a pawn being moved around by greater forces. It's a great big act, of course. Her and me. I watch her gaze slide off of me and fix on nothing in the room. She's already there. In Dubai. With Joe. A light comes into her eyes. She won't know it's there. Or that I can see it. It wasn't there a minute ago. When it was just the two of us. I wonder what she's seeing.

We're in bed now. Her back is turned and her knees are curled up in front of her. It's nearly midnight. Late for her. Early for me. But I've come to bed hopeful of a reward for my good behaviour earlier. Like a loyal dog sitting on the kitchen tiles staring eagerly at his cupboard. Go on. Throw him a bone. This one already has a bone. I stare at her back. The light is off but it's never completely dark in our room. We have thin curtains and there is a streetlamp outside. We toss and turn all night in this otherworldly, ethereal glow. She has freckles on her shoulders. Like all redheads probably. There was a time when I would kiss each and every one of them. She would fall asleep while I was doing it. I don't bother with that now. I don't bother with anything that might not come back to me in at least equal measure. I reach under the blanket and put my hand on her hip. The skin here is thin. It's pulled tight over the bone. If she gets goosebumps while I'm stroking her that's a good sign. Nothing yet. I move my hand around her. There is a little valley between her hip bone and tummy. She does have a tummy. A little round paunch. I like it. I put my head on it and hear it working away sometimes. Gurgling and breaking things down. Still no reaction. I move my hand back over her hip and onto her arse, rubbing it softly, feeling its shape in my palm. I give it a playful squeeze. Nothing. I especially like the fold where her buttock meets the top of her leg. My fingertips find it and trace along it. I'm being ever-so subtle. This is my best work in ages. After putting in the groundwork I move towards the middle. Not yet though. In one dextrous movement my fingertips lift off her skin and then land gently on the other side. They'll be back. At least I hope they will. This cheek feels different to the other one. It's because it has the weight of her body on it. It's pressed out more. Again I give her a little squeeze. It's mischievous. Fun. I'm hoping that's how she's taking it. She hasn't moved. I'm staring at the back of her head, trying to see through her skull to her face for a sign. Ever so slowly I begin to move my hand back the way it came. Towards the middle. The moment of truth.

'What are you doing?'

'Nothing.'

'I'm tired.'

'It won't take long.' This is true.

'I said I'm tired.'

I nearly say please but stop myself just in time. It seems to me that in every relationship, every bad relationship anyway, there is always one person who overshoots and one person who underachieves. This natural imbalance creates tensions that show themselves in a thousand different ways. What's happening now is just one of them, but every day we're confronted by the gap between what she wants and what I offer. It's always been there. It's put me on the defensive since the very beginning. Do you think I'm nice? Am I good-looking? I ask these questions of her every day. Don't be silly, she says. That's not an answer. I still don't know why she said yes. I half wish she hadn't.

I press myself up against her. I'm not small. I had a girlfriend once who called me a hoover. I didn't know what it meant. I asked my boss. He just stared at me. So I know I'm not small. She should be grateful.

'I'm horny,' I say.

'You do it then.'

In defence of Dolores, this isn't as dismissive and cruel as it may sound. It's actually a game we sometimes play. She likes to watch. And I don't mind her watching. It's a close second. And sometimes it leads to something else. You just never know your luck on a big ship.

'Should I?'

'If you want to. Just do it quietly.'

Okay. That part is as dismissive as it sounds. I can't dress that up. What I should do now is roll over and go to sleep. Accept your lot. Where's your pride, man? The problem is that the urge is in me now. It's been building all day. To this moment. It won't be ignored. My breathing is shallow. I have butterflies. I'm Pavlov's dog again. I realise my hand is still on her arse. That's something at least. I want to stroke it but I dare not in case she realises it's still there.

I close my eyes. I put my other hand under the blanket. I think of her in her pencil skirt and sheer blouse. We're in the tent again, the car, the pool. Real scenarios and imagined ones. She wants me in all of them. She doesn't turn around.

Chapter Eleven
Now

She's been dead for weeks. Why have I not snooped yet? There you go. That shows the respect I have for the old dear. But I'm only human. And she's long gone. They say you can't take it with you. I start in the main room.

'Just ignore me,' I say to her. She does. Not a murmur from the chair. But there is nothing here. I look in the drawers. All the compartments of the unit. I look under her mattress – plural, there are two of them, so that answers one question. I look behind the pictures for hidden envelopes and in her bedside cabinet. And his. I assume. But there really is nothing to get excited about. Nothing I can even concoct a story around. I go into the kitchen. In one of the drawers, just lying there, is a wad of notes. There is an elastic band around it. The top one is a fifty. I pick up the wad and thumb through it. They are all fifties. The wad is as thick as a deck of cards. I know this because there is a deck of cards in the drawer too and I hold them against each other. There are fifty-four cards in a pack. But bank notes are much thinner. Much thinner.

'And this, Flo?' I shake the wad at the back of her head. She ignores me. There must be close to £5,000 here. I put the money back and close the drawer. I'm no thief.

Her cupboard and chest of drawers are in the hallway. It's wide enough. I'm not surprised she hasn't thrown out Len's clothes. His shirts and slacks are in the cupboard. This is his socks and pants drawer. Something comes over me and I take a pair of his pants out and put them on my head. I walk back to where Flo is still seated and stand in front of her doing a silly jig and laughing. I stop suddenly. His pants disgust me and I take them off and throw them across the room.

I go into the bathroom. Two toothbrushes. A can of deodorant. For men. I don't recognise the label. I look for a sell-by date but can't find one. In front of me is the cabinet. Its door is a mirror. I'm staring at myself. I look a mess. Not untidy or unshaved. A mess on the inside. It shows on the outside in my expression. I feel like I want to cry for some reason. I try to, but nothing happens. My face just looks strained and unnatural. I stick my tongue out at myself. I make other faces. Surprised. Enraged. Insane. In orgasm. There is such a thing as the Hawthorne effect. It describes how we change our behaviour if we think someone is watching us. That's how I feel now. Like I'm being observed. It's just me and Flo here. And Flo is not really here, is she. Does the Hawthorne effect work if you're observing yourself? Maybe it does, if one part of you is observing another. Perhaps the almighty is here, spying on me with his all-seeing eye. I don't believe in all that. Sometimes I'd like to and try to pretend I do. But what Flo said about reincarnation makes more sense. So it can only be me. The Watcher. I'm the only one here. I want to look away but somehow I can't. Suddenly I start punching the mirror. I didn't plan to. I keep punching it until it's shattered and fallen to the floor.

The cabinet door has opened in the commotion, and inside

are her dentures, some bars of soap still in their wrappers, and her tablets. I pick up her tablets and walk back to the lounge.

'Remember these?' I say. I sit down next to her. 'I'm sorry. I got in the way, didn't I?'

I'm talking about what happened a month before she died, when I discovered her collapsed on the floor. She'd not been attending her plants when I returned from my swim. That's how I knew something was wrong. She would either be there or her door would be open and the landing would be full of the smell of bacon cooking. I'd put my head in the doorway and see her at the hob.

'Something smells good,' I'd say.

She'd smile apologetically. 'Only I've made far too much of it again.'

She never would just invite me in.

But one morning the door was closed and she wasn't by her plants. I noticed this only in hindsight. Only when she wasn't there the following day either. I walked into my flat and stood in the middle of the floor. I was waiting for the thing that felt wrong to reveal itself. It's odd how that happens. How our senses send instant messages to our brains, but our brains take their own sweet time to assimilate them. But eventually an image of the empty hallway and closed door popped into my head. I knocked on her door and when there was no response I got the key she'd given me months earlier 'just in case'. In case of what?

I didn't see her at first. She wasn't in her chair. She wasn't in the kitchen. The bed was made. But then I saw her. Half of her. The bottom half. Her legs were sticking out from behind the bed. Her nightie had ridden up over her knees to reveal white compression socks. Even from the doorway I could see her leg hairs squashed beneath the material. They were thick and black. Grotesquely so. She had soiled herself too. It had stained the cotton and left a smear across the floor, between her legs.

It wasn't until I was right up next to her that I realised she was alive. Her eyes were open and she was panting. Fast, shallow breaths. Futile breaths. Like something inside had shrunk or shut and the air wasn't getting all the way in. I thought of Reggie then. He used to breathe like that on hot nights. Our room was upstairs. It was the hottest room in the house. But he insisted on sleeping there. I told myself it's because I was there. I had tried carrying him down to the kitchen to let him sleep on the cool tiles, but each time he followed me dutifully back up the stairs. I'd listen to him panting at the foot of the bed, smiling to myself in the dark.

'Flo? Are you okay?' I squatted down beside her. 'What happened?'

She didn't answer me. Her eyes didn't move to show she had registered my arrival. She was staring straight ahead. At my feet. I noticed my toenails. They were long and thick. Disgusting. I tried to curl them into the carpet, out of sight.

'Flo?' I said again. I nudged her. Nothing. A sudden godlike sensation came over me then. Quite unexpectedly. It was almost overwhelming in its power. I looked down at her. For an instant I didn't see someone in desperate need of help, but someone helpless who was completely at my mercy. Here was another human being, another sentient life, and it was at my feet and totally and utterly powerless. I could do anything I wanted.

'Is it the same thing as last time?' She had had strokes before. Two that she knew of. There had probably been others. They don't have to always be severe. There is such a thing as a silent stroke. When the symptoms don't present. They can go undetected for months. For ever even.

'I will call an ambulance.'

She grabbed my ankle. She tried to say something. It was

just air coming out of her in a different way. I leant over her and put my ear to her mouth. She didn't say anything else. The first effort had exhausted her.

'I'll call an ambulance,' I said again. Her grip on my ankle tightened. Her eyes, flat and lifeless a moment earlier, were suddenly blazing. She lifted them up my body to glare at me. *Don't you dare*, they said. *Don't you even dare. You promised.*

It was because of Len. He died in hospital. He'd gone in healthy and never came out. It was meant to be routine. She told him cutting someone open was never routine. She said she didn't believe in cutting and that she'd never forgive him if he went. He went anyway. She shunned him the night before. He left in a huff. They never spoke again.

'Okay,' I said. 'No ambulance.' Her grip on my ankle loosened. Her fingers slid down my skin until her hand was limp on the floor. 'But I must do something.'

That's when I went to the bathroom to get her tablets. I thought it was probably too late, but I couldn't just sit there and watch. She coughed it out. Or spat it out. It sat on the carpet all soggy and drooled on. 'Now, Flo, you know it's good for you.' I picked it up and put it in her mouth again. I put my fingers all the way in her mouth this time so the tablet was on the back of her tongue. Then I held her jaw shut and massaged her throat, like I used to do with Reggie. I saw her swallow.

'Well done. That will do the trick.'

She closed her eyes on me. *Yes*, I thought. Too late. I watched tears form between her lids then roll silently down her cheeks. I took her hand in mine. I brushed her hair back. 'Shush,' I said. 'Shush, shush. It will be okay.' I didn't understand, of course. I thought, in my ignorance, that she was scared of what was coming. I thought that she had been dying in stages for years, probably ever since Len went, with parts of her life fading to nothing one by one, and that she recognised this as the final stage. I would stay with her. In her final hour. I won't say I looked forward to it. But I looked forward to how it would make me feel about myself again. Selfless. Noble. Heroic even. Like a superhero again. It had been so long. I took the blanket from the bed and laid it over her. I didn't call anyone. I laid down beside her. I closed my eyes and slept. I think now that this was a warm-up for me too.

'I'm still alive,' she said. It was the next morning. She was glaring at me.

'How?'

She told me later that she had been getting ready for bed when her chest suddenly closed like a clenched fist. Everything was squeezed and she couldn't breathe. She reached for something to steady herself on but her eyes couldn't see anymore and she missed. She hit the ground hard and lost consciousness. When she opened her eyes again she was staring out the window at an orange sky. She thought she was in heaven and was happy. Because the wait was over. But then she realised where she really was. And that she was still waiting. She stayed there for two days. She thought she could have made it to the bathroom if she tried, but she didn't try. She was determined to do nothing at all while the last of her strength drained away. I thought of myself beneath the water. I wished I had her resolve. She said she passed out many times but each time she came around again, and then it was morning and I was beside her and she knew the moment had passed. That was why she cried.

'I feel like I should apologise.'

She was propped up in bed. The tea I had made her was on the bedside table. Her hair was damp from the shower. I had carried her there. I had washed her when she refused to wash herself. I had kept washing her until the water circling the plug hole was clear.

'You don't need to apologise. But you owe me.'

I look at Flo just sitting there now, silently reproachful. I shake the bottle of tablets. It makes a loud sound in the deathly quiet room. But she won't even look at me.

'Come on now,' I say. I think she's being unfair. 'I only delayed you a month. I know you wanted to see him. But what's a month in the whole span of infinity? It's nothing at all. Flo? It's nothing.'

No, she is giving me the cold shoulder. I imagine this is the same haughty treatment poor Len got before his operation. I take her hand. The contact disgusts me but I don't let go immediately. I know what she's thinking. She's thinking that I knew what she wanted. When I discovered her there that morning. That I should have just walked away and left her to it. But she was my friend. It was asking too much. I couldn't be expected to carry that. I replace her hand gently on the armrest and walk to the door. I stop and look back. Len's pants are still in the corner. I pick them up and put them back in his drawer. I return the tablets to their bathroom shelf. At the door I stop again.

'It really was just a month,' I say to her. 'You got there in the end.' But she won't forgive me yet.

Chapter Twelve
Then

This is how it was...

7am: I wake up. I am probably hungover. Still groggy. I go downstairs, just, and make a coffee. I can hear Dolores in the shower. Grace is in the other room watching television, eating her breakfast. I sit at the kitchen table until I've finished the coffee then pour another one. I will have that after my shower.

'Morning, hero.' I stick my head through the doorway. 'I'm taking you to school again today.' Grace smiles and gives me a thumbs up.

8am: I am dressed. Shirt and tie. Sometimes a suit. Sometimes just smart trousers and a jacket. My brogues are downstairs by the door. All three of us are sitting at the kitchen table now. Dolores is on her phone, checking emails, sending messages. I ask Grace if she has everything she needs. If she's packed her lunch. If she needs a lift home.

Dolores looks up.

'Are you picking her up? I thought I was today.'

'No, it's fine. I can do it. Our meeting has been postponed.' She looks back down at her phone and resumes doing whatever it was she was doing. It's been a month since the boardroom. Just over. I've still not told her. I have no intention to now. I've applied for three other jobs. One said no. One hasn't come back to me. One invited me to an interview. It was yesterday. I didn't attend.

8.30am: All three of us walk out the door at the same time. This is rare. Dolores has usually gone before us. Sometimes even before I wake up. It's the Dubai trip. It requires an awful lot of preparation and research. She's working long hours. I'm still full of understanding.

'Goodbye, dear, love you.' This is Dolores to Grace.

'I'm not sure what time I'll be back.' This is Dolores to me.

Grace and I are in the car. There is a song playing that we both know and like. I deliberately get the words wrong. I sing *tired* instead of *trying*. It annoys her. I do it every time the song comes on.

'No! Just listen!' We both cock our ears to the radio. I'm trying very hard not to smile. As the line approaches we lean forward again. We're both mouthing the lyrics silently to each other. At the key moment I shout/sing 'Tired' over the singer singing 'Trying'.

'See? See? Did you hear? *Tired!*'

'Daddy!'

So it goes on. Until the next time the song is played.

8.45am: I walk Grace into school. I look at the mothers around me. There are two there I like. One is blonde. The other is an uglier version of Dolores. I resent the fact that I'm drawn to her. I've not managed to strike up a conversation with either of them. I'm not sure what I'd say. They are much younger than me. One has a wedding ring on. Who am I kidding? I'm just playing games in my head. Grace is practising her spelling as we walk. I'm paying full attention. When she gets a letter wrong I raise my eyebrows and she stops to reconsider.

'Good luck,' I say, and kiss her on the forehead. Yes, she really is quite ugly. I can't pretend she's not. I look at the other children in the playground and would say, objectively, that she is in the ugliest ten per cent. It makes me love her more. Her hair is tied up. Her socks are pulled up. She tucks her shirt in. She tries so hard. But you can't change it. I look challengingly at the other children. I'm daring them to say something mean.

9am–9.30am: I've been home to pick up Reggie. Now I'm driving out of town. I need to go far enough away so the chances of anyone I know recognising me are slim to none. My smoking paraphernalia is in the glovebox. In a blue folder that looks like something I'd have for work. It wouldn't interest Grace at all. There is a McDonald's on the way. I change out of my suit there, in the toilets. I put on jeans and a T-shirt. Weather-dependent. The bag with my spare clothes also includes a bottle of water. A packet of chocolate biscuits. A chocolate bar. Another chocolate bar. A packet of sweets. Sometimes I'll order a second breakfast at McDonald's. Not often.

9.45am: I'm parking up. I'm walking across the farmlands. I follow the same route every day. After about a mile you can't hear or see the road. You are over dale and far away. There is a ditch there, with a broken tree trunk across it. This is my destination.

10am–2pm: I am sitting on the broken tree trunk. I am smoking. I am looking all around me, taking in the world. There are no people here. Only traces of people. The things they've done. The crop lines through the field are arrow straight. There are pylons off in the distance. And wind turbines. Occasionally I can hear a train rumble by. Reggie returns every so often to make sure I'm still here. He comes right up to me, sniffs my leg, looks up at me with that smile of his, and then he's off again. Reggie is nine now. The same age as Grace. He was a gift from Dolores. It meant a lot because she had never wanted a dog. She had emphatically not wanted a dog. When she was young – she is still young, but I mean little girl young – a friend of hers was mauled by a dog. It left lasting scars. On her and her friend. So it was quite a gesture when she came back that Sunday afternoon with Reggie. He was only a puppy then. He's grown into a fine specimen. He follows me around the house. Whichever room I'm in he wants to be in. When I hide in the bathroom for half an hour he lies down on the carpet outside the door to wait. I think he'd starve himself at my graveside. He's brought me so much joy. I should thank Dolores again. Poor Dolores. I feel sorry for her. I must be such a let-down. I didn't expect her to say yes. I know I've said that before, but that's because of how true it is. And how much it's shaped us. Both of us. I was never going to live up to her expectations. It was unfair of her to ask me to. Each new day there are new reminders of what she wants and what I offer and what the gap is between the two. We both resent the situation. And this is even before she finds out about my dynamic walk to the door, my latest rebellion.

Reggie is here sniffing at the bag. He wants my biscuits. He can't have them. Dogs are so much less complicated than people. All animals are really. There is a robin on a branch. I've always liked robins. They're meant to be good luck. He is hopping from one spindly leg to another. For the record he's not red-breasted at all. It's rust. It's the colour of a rusted gate, with the sun on it. I've seen him before. He is always on that branch when I come here. Assuming it's the same one. I feel like it is. It's the wrong time of year for robins of course. He's either months early or months late. He's just another example of how things have been knocked out of kilter, of how we, our species, have knocked things out of kilter. I look at the crops where forests once grew. At the pylons, the wind turbines. I listen for the next train. I said humans were the plague, I really mean it.

Take us out of the equation and everything has its place, everything happens for a reason. One thing follows another thing, making the next thing possible. There's eight billion of us now. And the earth is no bigger than it was a million years ago. There's not enough to go around.

I wonder what the robin thinks? And all the robins. Walk into a clearing in the woods, watch the squirrels and rabbits scarper, watch the birds scatter from the trees. Swim in the ocean, notice the tiny fish dart in the opposite direction. They know what we are. What I am. I can't pretend I'm not. I stand up and walk slowly towards him. He stops twitching. My hand is outstretched. I'm making a weird cooing sound that doesn't sound like any bird I've ever heard. I'm three yards away. Two. It jerks its head in my direction and flies off. Yes, I know what I am. The animals rush from me, also.

I sit back down on the tree trunk. I smoke some more. I might lie down in the ditch and close my eyes. I will, sometimes, consider my current situation. It can't go on indefinitely. I don't know what's next. I don't worry about it. What will be, will be. I'm just waiting for it to happen. That's my job at the moment. That's what my gut is telling me to do right now. Nothing. Nothing apart from being open and ready to let happen to me whatever is divined.

2pm–2.45pm: Walking back to the car and driving back to town. I can manage driving now. My iron constitution is back. I stop at McDonald's again, but not to change back into my suit. I don't need to worry about that now. Just to drop the litter off. The water bottle and the wrappers.

2.45pm–3pm: Collecting Grace. Looking at the mothers. Two in particular. One of them has changed. The one who isn't married. The blonde. She is now wearing a denim skirt and pink top. She had jeans and a jumper on earlier. She looks even younger than she did. I need to be realistic. Grace's spelling test was a triumph. She got nineteen out of twenty.

'What happened with the one you got wrong?' I shake my head at her in mock disappointment. She punches me in the arm. It actually hurts but I don't let her see that.

3.15pm–3.45pm: I take Grace for an ice cream. We go to the same place every day. I order the same thing. A chocolate waffle with syrup and ice cream and other sweet things that I can't name. Grace has something different every day. She has gone through the menu twice.

'This won't last forever,' I say, 'so let's enjoy it while we can.'

'You need to tell Mummy.' Her serious reply catches me off guard. I see her mother's face in her. 'The longer you wait the harder it will be.'

I think that she is very wise for a nine-year-old. I wipe the ice cream off her lip and make a joke about it. Changing the subject.

3.45pm–7.30pm: I unpack my bag, putting my brogues back by the door and hanging my 'work' clothes over the chair in our room. I feed Reggie and cook dinner for the three of us. My repertoire has broadened. I'm surprised to discover that I enjoy cooking and am also reasonably good at it. I put tinfoil over Dolores' plate and Grace and I eat dinner at the table. She finishes before me. Which I don't understand as she does not stop talking while she eats.

'Don't talk with your mouth full, please.'

Perhaps it's because I have to stop to clean up whatever it is she has knocked over. She puts her pyjamas on while I take the dog for a walk. What I smoke now will have to see me through to bedtime. Grace's bedtime. Not mine. We then watch TV together while waiting for Dolores. Grace talks over it but I don't care. I am feeling the cushions beneath me. My eyelids are drooping. Reggie climbs on the couch with me and goes to sleep with his snout on my thigh.

7.30pm–8.30pm: I hear the door open and rouse myself, gather all my energy together for a perky greeting. Grace is taken to bed and for at least fifteen minutes Dolores and I sit on her bed while she reads to us. Reggie wanders in and paces. He doesn't like Grace's room. It's too hot and he can't get comfortable. Just as he settles down we kiss Grace on the forehead and walk out. He grumbles at our backs as we leave, and then drags himself after us.

8.30pm–10.30pm: Dolores has a shower and I watch the TV and wait for her. I hope she puts on her black nightie and I hope she doesn't. If she does put it on I will gawp at her surreptitiously. If she doesn't put it on I won't want her as much, and I won't end the night quite so frustrated.

10.30pm–1am: Dolores goes to bed. I use the next two or three hours to smoke as much as I possibly can before I follow her. I usually manage another four or five. It takes longer to roll them than it does to smoke them. The television is on but I am not watching. I am watching. But I'm not seeing.

1am: I get into bed. The last chocolate of the day is still in my mouth. Once I've swallowed it I'll lick my teeth and gums to get every last bit. I lay my head on the pillow and listen to Dolores beside me. When I am sure she's asleep I put my hand under the duvet. I will sometimes think of other women, but it's never as satisfying.

1.06am: I roll over and go to sleep. My last thought is not to scratch the tickling sensation running down my belly.

Chapter Thirteen
Now

I can hear knocking on the door. It's once removed. It's not my door. I put my head against it and listen. It's coming from across the landing. From Flo's door. I wish we had those little peepholes so I could see who's there. I listen carefully. Three knocks. Silence. Three more knocks. Much louder. They're angry knocks. A bell sounds. It's very quiet. Muffled. It's coming from inside Flo's flat. I didn't even know she had a bell. Then more silence. I press my ear against the door. Why do we pull faces when we're straining to hear? And our eyes move around, like they will see the sound. Suddenly the rapping is on my own door. I can feel it through the wood. I stumble backwards. As I fall I put my hands out to cushion my landing, so it's quiet. I find myself braced in the push-up position, holding my breath. Silence. I wait. I wait. They've gone. I still don't move though. Another knock. Not as urgent. I hear voices in the hallway. It's just one voice. I can't work out the words but the tone is not happy. It's a man's voice. Then there is silence again. My arms are already shaking. I'm not very fit. I've only been in this position for about thirty seconds. I'm actually sweating. It drops off my forehead and makes a dark spot on the carpet. I'm waiting for another drop, to see if it lands in the same place. I'm waiting but I'm also still listening. I must exercise. I lower myself onto the carpet. At eye level I can see all the individual threads. More silence. I begin to wonder if he's gone. Suddenly my door shakes on its hinges. That's how hard he is knocking. Or banging. Demanding. I listen carefully. It's not his knuckles. It sounds like he's made a fist and is hitting the door with the soft, fleshy bit underneath. Then it stops. Then he does the same to Flo's door. I'm still on the floor. I won't move. Another drop of sweat falls off me but I've moved so it lands somewhere else. There is a loud crash in the hallway. Something breaks. Heavy footsteps stomping down the stairs. The outer door opens then slams shut. Still I don't move. I listen. He's not coming back. I jump up and rush to the window. I'm just in time to see him getting in his car. I can only see the back of his head but I know it's him. Well. He finally came. I never thought I'd see the day.

'Do you want to take it?' I'm holding out the note Derek shoved under her door but Flo doesn't want to take it. She won't even look at it. 'Shall I read it to you, then?'

I turn it over in my hands. It's been scribbled on the back of a receipt. A coffee and a chicken and bacon sandwich. Nothing incriminating. I skim through it silently.

'Why does he call you Doris? Not Mum. Or Mother. He should call you Mother. That's what I imagine him calling you. Anyway. He says he's sorry he missed you. He came a long way out of his way to see you today.' I look at Flo and raise just one eyebrow. *This guy*, my eyebrow says. *Who is this guy?* She won't look at me, but she knows. 'He says he'll give you a call later.' I turn the receipt over again. Looking on both sides. Although I know there's nothing on the other side. 'That's all he says.'

I remember seeing a lighter somewhere in here. I wander around the room. There really is so little in here. You think of old people as hoarders. As collectors and repairers and storers of things that are no longer useful. But Flo's flat is sparse. There are two shelves on the wall that don't have anything at all on them. There is a photo on her bedside table. And a glass of water. Or just a glass. There is no water in it now. But almost nothing else. There is the lighter. On the floor by the bed. I look around again. Not even a candle. So why the lighter? What might she have been up to in here?

'Flo? You dark horse. Something you want to tell me?'

I'm just teasing her. I smile and shake my head at the back of her chair. I was much less forthcoming when she was alive. Less friendly. I was reticent and withdrawn. Do they mean the same thing? I was worried what she'd think of me. If she knew me. But I'm telling her things now. I've told her about Reggie. That was hard. Admitting that. I'd never said it out loud before. It brought it all back and made my stomach twist. I still can't believe... but anyway. Enough. Or I'll get all disturbed again.

In Flo's defence she's proven herself to be a good listener. Fantastic even. She hasn't judged me. I don't know what she really thinks about the stuff she's heard, but she's made it so I've not been afraid to tell her other stuff. I think that's the best you can hope for. I walk up behind her. I'm about to put my hand on her shoulder but stop myself just in time. I won't touch that. I sit down again and pick up the note. If the lighter doesn't spark in three flicks then I need to cut off my finger. Or Flo's finger. Just as Roald Dahl said. But it sparks first time. I wasn't really going to cut off my finger.

The note smoulders and then catches. In another second I've let it go and I am watching the ashes float in front of me. I blow hard and they shudder in mid-air, as though they don't know which way to go, and then scatter into nothing.

'He'll be back,' I say. 'Don't worry. We'll see him then. I'll ask him why he smashed up your pot plants. I'm not happy about that.'

Chapter Fourteen
Then

G race is crying. Dolores is holding her and looking over her head at me.

'I don't know,' I say. 'He was here. And then he just seemed to disappear.'

Reggie has gone missing. I am in no fit state to absorb this on an emotional level. How many have I smoked today? Too many. Double figures. But I realise it's bad. I realise I need to be alarmed but I can't get there. In the back of my mind I'm aware I'm going to hate myself for this inability to respond appropriately. It's going to add to the pain and the inevitable guilt.

'I don't understand how he could just disappear?'

It's early evening. We are standing in the kitchen. I tell them I have driven around for hours. I have been to all the places we normally go to for walks. I have asked the people I met who were walking their own dogs if they've seen a German Shepherd on the loose. I have even asked some people who weren't walking dogs. I have been to all the vets. I shake my head at them. *I'm at a loss*, the gesture says. I don't know what else I could've done.

The problem is that I have done none of these things.

We agree to go out again together now. It's summer. There is plenty of light. We have at least another three hours. The vets will be closed though. 'No, wait, there is a twenty-four-hour surgery that we can try. I was there earlier,' I tell them, 'but it can't do any harm trying again.'

We are driving down one road and up another. Sometimes, when there is a patch of green, we all get out. I hear Grace calling his name. Her small voice that won't travel far. I call out too. I almost believe he could at any moment appear from inside a hedge and come running up to us as though nothing has changed.

'Has he got a tag?' someone asks. They heard us calling.

'Yes.'

'I'll keep an eye out.'

We thank them and move on. Down another road, to another patch of green. We should have had him chipped. We kept meaning to. Grace is more upset than I expected her to be. She has hardly stopped crying. I keep giving her water. I hear myself saying, 'He'll turn up, don't worry.' Over and over I say it to her. Dolores is devastated too. I didn't think she even liked the dog. I thought she might be secretly relieved. Maybe she is, and this is just for show. I don't believe that. She is the one organising the search. She has her business head on. She is so practical. So calm and methodical. I watch and admire. We go here. Once we've been there we go somewhere else. Once we've been there we go somewhere else again. She has a map out. She is marking the roads we've been down in red ink. I glance over and see the way the red is slowly moving left to right across the page. There are no gaps.

'I'll go in,' I say. We've come to the twenty-four-hour surgery. They are grateful I've volunteered to do this part. I go inside. The reception area is empty. There is a large scale on the floor and a water bowl. The woman behind the counter is looking at me. I get on the scale then pull a face at the woman.

'It must be the heavy shoes,' I tell her. I smile. She is young. Brown, straight hair. A little plain-looking. But they're the types that can surprise you.

I come out the surgery and shake my head at the two hopeful faces looking at me through the car window. We go on. I didn't realise the town was as big as it is. Our headlights are on now. The streetlamps have come on too. But we can still see through the last of the twilight. We go on. My phone rings. Everyone stops breathing and looks at me. I answer it. *Poe cheese? Big bags?* I shake my head at the girls again. 'No,' I mouth. He never phones me. I normally have to ask. 'Okay,' I say, 'thank you. Appreciate the call.'

It's dark when we finally get home. Grace has exhausted herself and is nearly asleep. I carry her up to bed, shoes and all. She asks me where he could be. 'Don't worry,' I say, 'he'll turn up.' Dolores is standing in the doorway watching. She has questions. I can see it on her face. But she's thinking now is not the time. He was here. And then he just seemed to disappear.

The next day is Saturday. We have printed out posters. More than 200. The poster is a picture of Reggie under the word 'missing' in big red letters. Our phone number is at the bottom of it. Dolores has flown to Dubai now. She left first thing in the morning. We had to promise to keep her updated. It's just Grace and me now. We are pinning the posters on lamp-posts and asking shop owners if we can stick them in their windows. It takes nearly all day. No one that we speak to has seen him. It doesn't make any sense. Grace and I are both confused. It's so unlike him.

'He must be so hungry.'

'If I know Reggie, he'll have found something to eat somewhere. He won't go without his food for long.'

Grace nods. She tries hard to believe me. I'm trying that myself. When all the posters are gone we return home. I check my phone to see if anyone has left a message. I text Dolores that there is nothing to update. The posters are all up and now we're just waiting. Grace wants to go and search again. She wants to go further afield this time. Out of town. I want to go to that rotting gate again and forget all of this. I loved Reggie more than either of them did. It's not easy keeping this grief at bay. I tell Grace that it's a good idea and we get back in the car and drive out of town. We're surrounded by farms again. I have no idea which direction to go. There are little lanes everywhere. But it makes no difference. I turn up one and drive for half a mile before pulling over.

'Let's try here,' I say.

We walk to the top of a hill. It's not a large hill but it affords us a panoramic view in every direction. We stand there for about ten minutes, circling, squinting, looking for movement. We see sheep. Plenty of rabbits. At one point we think we see him, but it's a deer. He'd have loved it here. He'd be in his element. I should have brought him here. Grace is crying again.

'Let's go home,' she says.

'Don't worry. He'll turn up.'

Chapter Fifteen
Now

S ome days are better than others. Today is not such a good day. And the sun hasn't even come up yet. Perhaps it was seeing Derek. The back of Derek. Actually, seeing the back of Derek wouldn't be so bad. But his presence on the other side of my door made him real to me in a way that he hadn't been until then. And if he's real then everything else must be too. It's a shame. I was enjoying pretending that it was just me and Flo.

Yes, some days are better than others and today, Day 1,866, is not so good. I'm not aware of waking up. I am just aware that I am sitting in the chair and wondering what Grace would be up to at this very minute. I guess she's asleep. The time difference to where she is now is only an hour. I can't be sure if they're ahead or behind us, but it is so early that whichever way it is I am certain she is still asleep. She used to sleep under her duvet. I mean right under it. With it pulled up over her head. I wonder if she still does. She's fourteen now. Fourteen. How tall will she be? Has she got spots on her face? I wonder if she's growing into her face better. It's not Derek. Fuck Derek. Fuck him. It's her being fourteen that has made it into a bad day before it has even started.

I get off the chair and leave the flat. I should have fixed the pot plants. Or replaced them. I wouldn't have had to if Derek hadn't broken them. I notice the chicks in the chimney watching as I cross the road. There are no cars at this time of the morning. Everything is empty. I like it like this. It's like an apocalyptic world. Things left behind. The cans, the chip packets, the burst plastic football lying there in the sand with its face caved in. Eight billion. And counting. Or breeding. My spirit sags further. We can't be controlled. That's what I think. As a species. We'll just keep spreading and spreading and killing everything we come into contact with.

The seagulls are making all kinds of noise this morning. They seem to be in a mood. Disturbed about something. Maybe it is me. My presence. The animals rush from me also. One of them is standing in my path, glaring at me. He won't move. I walk towards him but he doesn't budge. He opens and closes his wings. Opens and closes his beak. But soundlessly. He doesn't squawk. It is spooky. Eventually I stop and we just stand there, about ten yards apart. I think if seagulls were twice as big as they are they'd take over the earth. I've heard stories about them snatching small dogs and cats. I can quite believe it.

'I'm your friend,' I say to this one now. 'I'm on your side.' But he doesn't believe me. He hops about on his twig-legs, looking mean. I walk towards him. As I pass he jabs his beak at me, making me jump sideways.

The tide is out. There is about 300 yards of beach before the water. The sand is soft then hard then soft again. I marvel at things like this. Things I don't understand. It must have something to do with currents and tides, but I can't explain it. I have so little knowledge about the world around me. I fail it. I am maybe halfway across the beach when I notice that I am not alone. There is someone else here this morning. Standing at the water's edge. It is just a silhouette from this distance, a black shape with its hands on its hips, but it is enough to disturb my equilibrium. I stop for a moment to consider. I survey the sea. There are no tankers. No fishing boats. Perhaps they are all on the other side of the head. There is nothing but that orange buoy bobbing about and somewhere beneath the waves the remains of a shipwreck. I didn't acknowledge Flo this morning. She's becoming a little too ghastly. I look back at the figure. It hasn't moved. I decide to continue with caution. And consternation. I understand how the seagull felt.

As I get closer I am able to make out that it's a man. But not just any man. A strange man. Strange is maybe a little judgemental. Peculiar then. That is softer. He is wearing denim shorts and a white crop top. In between the two, clearly visible, deliberately so, is a red G-string nestled in the hair of his lower back. He turns as I approach. He doesn't seem surprised. I wonder if he saw me before I saw him. He nods and I nod also but I don't stop. I don't want to engage. I want to pretend he's not even here. I walk quickly into the water. It's cold but I don't hesitate. I have a mission. I wade out up to my knees, my thighs, my waist. Gradually it's getting shallower again. Sandbanks. The seabed rises under me and lifts me out of the water to my knees again. I want to swear but I don't want him to hear me. I turn around. He's still within earshot. He is watching me. At least it looks like he is. I can't see his eyes. He's looking in my direction though. Behind him I can see that same seagull. He's followed me to the water's edge. I just know it's him. And behind him, far, far away now, is the promenade and the houses, mine and Flo's, and the window through which she is urging me on. I wave at her. The man waves back. There are no gestures I can think of to signal that I meant someone else. I want to swear again.

I turn around and keep going. The water reaches my chest. Then my neck. When a swell rolls in it lifts me off the bottom for a moment before placing me down softly on the sand again. I wonder if Virginia Woolf went even deeper. I think this will do though. I lift my hands out of the water and stroke the surface. In front of me the sea just drifts off into a haze and comes out the other side as sky.

I take a deep breath then lift up my feet. I'm instantly in another world. It's completely silent apart from the internal hum of silence itself. Soon the seabed bumps gently into my crossed legs. I blow out a mouthful of air, sinking me down onto it. And now I wait. My mission this morning is to see how long I can stay under. I mean if I really try. If I'm totally committed. I want to get to the point where the decision is taken out of my hands. Every time there comes a stage when I can't hold my breath any longer and I jump up into the air. I want to go beyond that. It's like falling asleep. Apparently. My mind always wanders when I try to fall asleep.

I can't decide if Flo would be proud of me or not right now. I could never really work her out. Which is strange because I think she only ever told me the truth. I, on the other hand, hardly ever told her the truth. I'm honest with her now. But while she was alive I think I must have told her fewer truths than untruths. Despite all that, though, I think she had my number. She never said much about it. But she knew more than she let on. She thought my name was Hank. I told her that. I don't know why I lied.

'Doris?' I said. 'I can't imagine you as a Doris. I've always thought of you as Flo.'

'Call me Flo then.' That's when she told me about past lives and why she thought people got names wrong. 'What's your name?'

'I'm Hank.'

I don't know a Hank. I don't think I ever have. It's not exactly a name that jumps up at you. The only Hank I can think of now is Hank Williams. My father used to listen to him. He sung bluegrass. But I can't think of a single one of his songs.

Flo looked at me sceptically. I think she was sceptical. Maybe it was just my guilty conscience. 'I'll call you Hank then. If you like.'

If you like. Now why did she add that if she believed me? There were lots of little asides like that. I can't remember them all but they've created the impression in me that she didn't believe much of what I said but wasn't the sort to pry. I sometimes wish she had. It might have lifted a weight had I opened up and confided in her. It was never a lack of trust. I knew I could trust her. That she'd not judge me harshly. But after the first lie, the others just came naturally. No, never married. No kids either. That was like stabbing myself. No pets. Another blade going in. I made it all up. I was a whole new person by the end. I much preferred him to me.

'Whenever I want to put rocks in my pocket and walk out into the water I go and take care of the plants.' This was Flo. Disarmingly honest. 'They are the only living things that rely on me.'

I realise now that she said it for my benefit. I didn't realise at the time. I thought she was just done with the world and holding on a little longer. But it was for me. For when she was gone. That's why it was such a bad sign when Derek smashed them up.

I can't do it. It feels like there is a bubble inside me getting bigger and bigger and bigger. Any moment now the pressure is going to burst open all my orifices. I can feel the sand against my toes. I just need to push off it. My head is throbbing. I can hear it in my ears. I'm going to open my mouth and try to breathe. I can't not. The prospect of sucking in that seawater, gulping as fast as I can but more and more and more rushing in is too terrifying to think about. I put my feet down and shove upwards. I inhale a fraction too early and break the surface coughing and spluttering. But just like that I've failed again and it's over for another day. I'm relieved and I'm not relieved. Tomorrow then. I regain my composure and look for him on the shore. He's not there. Good.

I wade in and begin walking back. I don't know how they did it. Mrs Woolf and co. But then they had the advantage of being ill. The sun is just up now. I can feel it warm on my wet skin. The litter is all still here. Even more than I first noticed. Maybe I will come back with a black bag. That can take the place of the pot plants.

I'm still considering this when the strange man steps out from the shadow of the promenade. I immediately stop. He's naked. No. Not quite naked. He has on his red G-string. The front of it is nothing more than a pouch. Not a very big pouch. I've never liked G-strings. Not on women. Regardless of their shape. And now I'm looking at it in the flesh so to speak I don't like them on men either.

He raises his hand tentatively. I think it's a wave. I can see him better now than before. A little too much of him. He has too much skin for his body. Or his body doesn't have enough solid things to fill it up. It sags, bits of him hang over other bits, making ugly folds in his chest, his arms, his hips, even his legs, around his knees especially. And everything seems too long for him, like he's a short person attached to a tall person's limbs. He knows this. You can see the way he stands. Awkwardly like that. Stooping. Letting everything droop. Even his hair just hangs straight down. He's like a human weeping willow. I've seen enough. I turn to leave.

'Wait. Please.'

I hesitate. He sees me hesitate and beckons me over.

'Please.'

I know I should leave. Something is stopping me. Something makes me want to go over there. Maybe it's just curiosity. He looks along the beach. One way then the other. I look too. There is no one around. Just us.

He waves me over again.

My toes are crunching the white sand. It's soft here. They close around something hard that is lying just below the surface. I pull it clear. A dried-up starfish. That seagull will have this later. The strange man's hands are on his hips again. The same pose he had down at the water. He nods. I tell myself he might be in some sort of trouble. Maybe he wants me to help him. I know it's not true, but it makes it easier for me to lift up my foot and take the first step.

Up close I realise he's even older than I thought. He has much more hair on his ears than I do. He even has it growing out of his ears. And sprouting from his shoulders. I remember his lower back. I bet he has a whole rug. Old Silverback. He turns around to prove me right. I didn't need proof. I didn't want it. He leans forward from the waist and starts patting his backside. I can't help myself. I look. It is white. It stands out starkly against the sun-beaten skin on his legs and waist. It is pockmarked with cellulite too. I'm no connoisseur, but I'm not impressed. I want to look away, but my eyes linger unwillingly.

He is watching me over his shoulder. He raises his eyebrows. It's a question but I don't know what he's asking. I don't know the rules here. I don't know what the signals mean. I just stare back. He looks hurt. Almost scared. Or vulnerable. That's the exact word. I detect a tiny shake of his head. I offer a reassuring smile. *It's not you, it's me* – but it most definitely is him. But my smile cheers him right up and he turns around and pulls me to him. 'Oomph,' I say, as my chest bounces into his. I am surprised at the force of it, and how tight he holds me. His skin is hot. The sun is still weak but he is sweating. He whispers something. I feel it in my ear more than I hear it.

'Sorry?'

'I said is this okay?'

'Umm...'

'Good.'

We just stand here. My arms are dangling by my side. I feel stupid like this, like I'm some kind of life-sized puppet. I put them around him. I can feel the hair between my fingers. I am a little disgusted with all this. With myself. I find it nearly appalling. But I'm conflicted too. I can't pretend a part of me hasn't craved this. I begin to calculate how long it has been since I held anyone. Since anyone held me. Grace would have been the last. We're talking years. I didn't realise how much I missed it. I'm not a tactile person, but human contact matters as much as food and water and shelter.

He moves his arm from my back and pushes it between us. He starts rubbing my stomach with a flat hand and I instinctively arch away from him. He takes it as an invitation. He thinks it means I'm giving him room. That's not what I meant, but without hesitation he puts his hand deep into my shorts.

'Yes?' he asks.

I can't speak. I am a fourteen-year-old girl who is letting her boyfriend do things to her that she doesn't want. But I'm letting him do them anyway because I want what comes with this more than I don't want this. I sort of sink onto his shoulder. He's fiddling around with me but I'm not paying any attention. I almost want to laugh. This is so absurd. What will I tell Flo? I didn't plan it. It just happened. He's still tugging at me but getting no reaction. I feel vaguely guilty. Like I'm letting him down.

I hear myself apologise. 'Can we just hug?'

He takes his hand away and puts it back around me. This is better. We just stand here again. I don't know for how long. I'm horrified to discover I've started crying. I can't help myself. I do it quietly. I just let the tears roll out of me. I don't want him to know. But he must know because they're dripping off my chin onto his back. Eventually he lets me go and takes a step backwards. He smiles. I don't know what I do. I'm walking back across the sand. That's all I know. The chicks are still there on the chimney top. *Squawk, squawk,* they say. One of their parents is with them now. Looming over them. Glaring at me. I'm certain it is the one from the beach again.

Chapter Sixteen
Then

This is cosy. It's just Dolores and I facing each other over the dinner table. There is soft lighting and soft music. But I'm not expecting anything later. Last week she let me go down on her and then was generous enough to give me a milking in return. As a thank you. So that's us for a month or so. She looks good though. Her hair is up, as I like it. When she moves a loose strand floats over her ear. I can see her neck, and the feminine hollow behind her collarbone. All these little things I notice about her. And appreciate. My attention is wasted on her though. Dolores. The hottest girl in school. The hottest and the coldest.

We've just had a wonderful dinner of lamb shanks and fresh vegetables. My palate feels cleansed and healthy. Through the window on my right, her left, I can see miles and miles of sky. It's grey. There is rain about but it's impossible to make out individual clouds. We're blessed to live where we do. It's a big property, near to town but far enough away to be quiet and give you that feeling of being apart from the hustle and bustle. In the mornings, with the windows open, you'll hear birds. Not cars. There is a golf course directly across the road so unless they sell up there is always going to be a vast green space alongside us. Green land. Green trees. Green bushes. When the sun goes down we can sit where we're sitting now and look at the shadows gathering in the swales and dips of the fairways. Rabbits run amok. If it sounds idyllic that's because it is. We're very lucky. We can't afford to live here. We could barely afford it when I was working. Dolores liked it though. She said it was perfect for hosting. I imagine her saying that, anyway. So she as good as said it. I don't know what we'll do now. I'm not sure how many mortgage payments we'll make before things start to unravel. I need to think about these things but I don't even want to. I'm still trusting to fate. Something will happen.

'I've just realised something.' That's Joe talking. His voice is so low I feel it vibrate in my stomach. If he keeps talking I'll want to do a shit. I clench my sphincter. I think the strain shows on my face and he looks at me a little oddly. He is standing in the doorway. Blocking it. His head touches the top. His shoulders brush the sides. He's been working out. All night I've been waiting for an opportunity to make a comment about lending him a T-shirt if he likes, one that fits. 'You must be awfully uncomfortable,' I hear myself saying. Every now and then his pectorals twitch. Or he deliberately flexes them. Dolores and me both notice. It's impossible not to.

'You were gone a while,' I say.

'That's because my piss has a long way to travel.' He winks at me. He doesn't really. And he didn't say that either. He ignores me. He says instead that what he's realised is that he's not seen Reggie tonight.

'I miss my dog.' He says this. Not me. My dog. He looks around his ankles, as though that's where he expects Reggie to be, belly up, fawning. The sad truth is that if Reggie was here that is exactly where he would be. The very first time Joe came to our house Reggie attached his snout to his feet and wouldn't be parted. I slipped away to the kitchen for some dog biscuits which I placed surreptitiously about my person, but it made no difference.

'Come on, boy,' I said. I patted my thigh. I tried to show him the biscuits without them noticing. He wouldn't come. I laughed it off. Joe said that he could probably smell his mother's dog. That's what it was. Ever so gracious. I seethed silently all night. When he'd gone and we were finally alone Reggie tried to make it up to me, but I was having none of it. I kept pushing him away until he got the message and slunk off to cool down on the kitchen tiles.

'Is he with Grace?' Joe is still going on about it. Dolores doesn't answer. She stares at me. I'm designated spokesman in the case of Missing Dog. I was the last person to see him after all. He was there and then he just disappeared. She's looking at me in a way that makes me feel guilty.

'So Dolores tells me Dubai went well.'

Joe looms over the table before lowering his physical presence into his chair. The problem I have is that I can't help liking him. Everyone likes him. When he's gone I quickly grow to despise him. The very idea of him. Or maybe it's only the idea of him. But then he's back and I find myself warming to him within minutes. I don't know what it is about him that attracts you. I think it's genuine though. That's the real sickener. He tells us, but mainly me, a story about a public garden in Dubai where workers walk around with whistles that make bird sounds. He says it makes you think you're in a tropical wonderland. He says it shows that there are no lengths they won't go to, to make a good impression.

'Sounds a bit shit,' I say. I hear Dolores sigh.

It's always like this. Whatever he says I try to discredit, dismantle, dismiss. Even if I agree with it. He must get bored of it. I know I do. That doesn't mean I'll stop it though. I say that I could never get on with the culture in Dubai. I'm too liberal, too much in favour of women's equality – another sigh – too open-minded. He tells me it's remarkably tolerant there now. Almost international. He wonders if I'm not mistaking it for Riyadh. But that's understandable because anyone who hasn't been to the Middle East is likely to bind everything up together. I say that the heat must be unbearable. He says how air conditioning in every single public and private space means you're often cooler there than here. I make a non-committal gesture to show I'm not convinced.

'Sandstorms,' I say. I'm getting desperate in the face of his relentless positivity. He's like one of those balloon figures that you push over and they just keep popping up again.

It's dark out the window now. The wine has gone. Or my wine has gone. Their glasses I notice are still half full. I top up. I tip the neck towards them and they both put their hands over their glasses.

'More for me then.'

They are talking shop now. I'm looking from one to the other. I'm looking at both mouths moving. Following the conversation like it's a physical thing passing between them. I try to keep track of the words but I'm not interested enough. I wonder what I'd do if I caught them in bed together. It shocks me to realise that the truth is I'd probably do nothing. I'd probably hold up my hands and say, 'Fair enough. I can't blame you. Either of you.' Then I'd slink away from them like Reggie slunk away from me. I'm sure they are having an affair. Why wouldn't they be? All those nights away from home. In five-star hotels. Five-star menus. Dressed to the nines in dinner suits and dresses. What happens on tour stays on tour. I'd like to have an affair. I would, too. If anyone would have me. How do these things start? I haven't a clue. Maybe one of the mothers at Grace's school. Or her teacher.

What's the first step, though? Do I accidentally brush my fingers against theirs? Do I just come out and say it? *Fancy a fuck?* I wouldn't know the words. I fill up my glass again. They still haven't touched theirs. I look up at their faces. They're so involved. So absorbed in what the other is saying. What am I doing here? Would either notice if I slipped down my chair and fell asleep on the floor beneath the table? The new Reggie.

I think the blonde would be better in bed. Gentlemen do prefer blondes. This gentleman does. I make a vague pact with myself to approach her. If I can get a conversation going then my natural sense of humour will come through. Isn't humour the most potent aphrodisiac? Dolores starts laughing. I gaze up. Joe is laughing too. I try to think back. Was it me? Did I just say something funny? I laugh too but I'm not sure why. I fill up my wine glass again. Not all the way this time because the bottle is empty. I see there is another bottle on the table. I pick it up. That one is empty too.

Joe lifts his glass to me and smiles over it. He says something that is friendly and well-intentioned. I smile back at him. I look at Dolores. She isn't smiling. At least she's looking at me. That's an improvement.

'What? What's wrong?'

I bet Joe could pay the mortgage on this house. He could probably buy it outright. But maybe not. If he can't even afford a shirt that fits. I laugh properly now. They stop and stare at me. It takes me a moment to realise that I didn't say that out loud. I sort of shake my head to say, *carry on, nothing to see here.* Yes. Joe could buy this house. Maybe I'll ask him to pay the mortgage for us. Just for a month or two. I look at him. So upright. So responsible. Grace would prefer him for a dad. That much is obvious. He looks at me. But he wouldn't be as much fun. He wouldn't let her have the day off school and take her out and buy her ice cream. I realise they're both looking at me now. I take a sip of my drink but there's nothing there.

'Are you going to answer him?'

'Sorry,' I manage. 'What was that?'

'I asked how your job is going. I'm sorry for talking about the business all night. I realise how boring it must be to an outsider. How's your work?'

That little kernel. It's suddenly back. The one from the boardroom. The one that only comes along when something unplanned and with an uncertain outcome is about to happen. How is my job going? That's what he wants to know. Well, well. Should I? Is now the time? Now's not the time. No time like the present though. I look at Dolores. She looks away from me at Joe and starts talking to him. He starts talking back. This annoys me. Annoys me far more than it should. *Hello? Hello? I'm over here.* Am I over here, or have I slipped under the table already? Maybe that's why they're carrying on as if they were alone. I slap myself in the face. That stops them. *Yes. Thank you. Here I am.* That kernel is a stone. Even harder and larger and more irresistible than last time.

'I've quit,' I say.

'What?'

'My job. I quit.'

'Fuck. Fucking hell.'

'I walked out.'

'For fuck's sake. I knew you'd pull a stunt like this.' She's paying me attention now. Now Joe is the one who might as well not be here. 'When?'

'About a month ago.'

'Fucking hell,' she says again. I like it when she swears. It gives me a cheap thrill.

'Didn't I say?'

There is a third bottle on the table. I have no idea how it got there. It's already open and I fill up my glass and drink it all in one bold effort. For a moment all sorts of heavy things shoot up into my head and it's hard to hold it still on my shoulders. I put my hands on the table to stop me toppling over. It's started raining. I knew it would. The raindrops are pounding into the glass. I've always loved a storm. It makes me want to be out there, braving the elements. Getting back to basics. I had a friend once who was struck by lightning. Twice. Incredibly he got up and walked away. True story. The pavement beneath his feet was burnt black but he was unharmed. It was something to do with his shoes. The type of soles they had. The current just passed right through him. We called him Same Place after that. It was a joke about lightning striking the Same Place twice. I pour more wine. I offer the glass to Joe. But Joe's gone. I look at Dolores.

'Top-up?'

'What have you been doing all day? When you've been pretending to be at work.' She stands up. She looks suddenly sad. 'Honestly, Adrian. I just don't know anymore.'

She never calls me Adrian.

'Don't be like that.' She's walking away. I stand up to follow her. I totter. 'Dolores. Wait. Let me–' My stomach lurches and shoves chunks of lamb shank, fresh vegetables and nearly two bottles of wine out of my mouth. I look at it seeping down my comfortably-fitted shirt. That's all I remember.

Chapter Seventeen
Then

J ust lying here in the sun. Warmth from above and warmth from below. Sometimes asleep, sometimes only half asleep. Just lolling about on the patio decking. It's a sun trap. The wood heats up in late afternoon. Like hot coals. My arm draped over my eyes. My other arm tucked under my head. There are boxes in the house. Full of clothes and pictures and plates. Other stuff. I acknowledge the thought then let it drift out of my mind again. *Later. Later.* I yawn. There is sweat on me. Not from any effort. Under my arms and in the small of my back. It cools when the air stirs. The air never stirs. Sometimes it rouses itself, moves somewhere nearby, then settles down again. That's all it does. Like an old dog. Dee is here too. On the sun lounger. Blue bikini. Legs and arms akimbo. Unless she's moved. But she's not moved. That is her calf my fingers are curled up against.

'We should have a baby.'

That was her. Maybe an hour ago. I said okay. We both drifted back to languor. Sensuously satisfied. I never want to move from this spot.

'I love you.'

'I love you.'

Evening now. On the couch. Tracksuit bottoms and vest. Her. Not me. Her comfortable clothes. No need to dress to impress anymore. I like the way she's let her guard down so soon. It says something about us. I don't know what exactly. I think it's a good thing though. She will leave the bathroom door open soon. Her feet are in my lap and I'm pressing my knuckles into the soft fleshy bits. She gathers stress in her feet. That's what she says. Every so often she yelps and jerks her foot away. That's when I know I'm doing it right. I go straight back to that spot.

Why did she marry me? That's what I want to know. It's our anniversary in five days. It doesn't make sense to me yet.

I'm telling Dee how much I'm looking forward to starting my new job tomorrow. It's a big fat lie. I'm not looking forward to it at all. I still can't believe I got it. Perhaps they mistook my disinterest for quiet confidence. We were in the car when they phoned. I put them on speaker. There's Dee clapping her hands silently at me while I try not to look at her. She was proud of me. She knew I could do it. I'd have said no had she not been there.

Jason Gash. That is his name. My new boss. I hate that word. *Boss*. He is my boss. He bosses over me. He tells me to do stuff and I must do it. No one is the boss of me. That's what I think. He is the boss of me. That's what everyone else thinks. Gash, though. Gash. No wonder he told me to call him Jason.

'Let me give you some advice for free,' he said, 'don't ask for permission first, ask for forgiveness later.'

His exact words. I can't wait to spend my days with him.

'It's only a name,' Dee says. She has delicate feet. Long and slender. Like her calves. But thick toes. Fat stubby digits that don't belong to her. She has disowned them. She never paints them. She bites their nails. It's quite something to see. I find a soft area and press. I lean my shoulder into it. As hard as I can. So much energy going through my thumb it looks disjointed. But it's here somewhere. That pressure point. Suddenly she squeals and pulls her foot back.

I want to know why she married me.

I watch her now without her knowing. I watch her when she's watching TV. As she is now. I watch her getting dressed. I watch her when she eats. So meticulous. She eats food off her plate by the colour. It should be me who does that. I can't start now though. It would just be copying. I watch her when she is on her phone, when she's entering or exiting a room, when she's walking to or from her car. It only counts if she doesn't know I'm watching. I watch her and I'm mesmerised. Mesmerised and perplexed. Mostly perplexed. What is she doing here? What can her long-term strategy be?

'Why did you marry me?'

'You kept asking.' She answers without missing a beat, without even moving her eyes from the screen. She's not surprised by the question. She has asked it herself. I don't say anything and the silence eventually reaches her. She does look at me now. Her manner softens.

'Aw, I didn't mean it like that.' She puts her hand on my knee and gives it a quick squeeze. 'I mean you're very determined. That's an extremely attractive quality in a man. It makes me think you might do great things one day.'

She smiles. *There, that should satisfy him.* That's what her smile says. Or it could be genuine. Just a normal smile. She continues watching TV. I continue watching her without her knowing. *You don't love her. You never have and never will.* The thought arrives suddenly, fully formed. It is alarming. Luckily it's not true.

I realise something quite marvellous. She's right. About great things and that I will one day do them. It makes perfect sense to me. I've never quite been able to pinpoint the source of my general agitation, but that's it. I am destined for something spectacular and the mundane is just holding me up. Now I think about it, I think I've always known this. Some people are set apart from the rest. With unusual qualities. Hidden qualities. Qualities that lie dormant, disregarded, until the supreme moment arrives.

There is something forming in my stomach. A little kernel of something. I recognise it as excitement. I want to know what they are, these qualities of mine, and what is coming that will draw them out. I so seldom feel equal to Dolores. But she sees something. Now I see it too. I will show the world.

Dolores is clicking her fingers at me. She has an odd expression on her face.

'What are you grinning about over there? You were miles away. Were you thinking about what I said?'

'Yes. I was actually.'

'You're sure? It's not too soon?'

'Too soon?'

'To start a family.'

What is she talking about? Oh. That. 'No,' I say, 'it's not too soon.' It's four days until our anniversary. Not five. That would be an ominous start.

'Good.' She wriggles her toes. 'Now focus on the arch.'

Salad days. An odd phrase. From Shakespeare. I know this. But I don't know how I know this. These are them. Right now. Rare I think to recognise them while they're happening. Not to have to look back wistfully. We were happy then. If only we'd known it.

Chapter Eighteen
Now

D ay 1,872. On an objective level it's actually quite marvellous what is happening to Flo. And has already happened. Of course, she's not Flo anymore. She's completely unrecognisable from the kind old dear who used to sit there gently ignoring me. Everything she was is long gone. That's why I can talk about it finally. About the physical process. It's impersonal now. She is Doris again. Doris Broadbent. Surely not. She was never her. She is nothing more than a corpse, a picture that I know will one day sit in a folder on a detective's desk. I never knew her.

It's been quite fascinating to see. A study in human evolution and the transience of a single existence. I have read up on all this. I've done my homework so I can attribute the correct terms to the various processes. I'll get to all that in a bit. But I must say, what I've read seems a little irrelevant. All the words we've created to explain things. It just seems petty. Small-minded. Like we've been so absorbed in the details we've missed the broader point. But that's us all over. Clever but not wise. Clever but without the necessary insight to use our cleverness for the greater good. Towards a greater understanding. This is sounding almost existential now. I have to admit, I never thought I'd have cause to use that word. But how can I not when what I'm talking about is the end of life.

But it's only the end of one kind of life. Because what I've learned from what I've seen over the last five weeks is that we never die. Not really. I'm not talking about the soul, the essence of our being, any of those spiritual vagaries which may or may not be there. We can claim to know the answer. Many do. But I don't believe any of us will ever truly know what's what until the old hammer comes down on us, finally and terminally. Until then it's all just conjecture and supposition. No, what I'm talking about is the actual body. It's the body that never truly dies. At least, not in the way that we view death. As a physical ending. A full stop. As something that is, becoming something that was. That is no more. In fact, death doesn't stop the body. The body just keeps going. I am starting to understand that it just keeps going for ever. For as long as there is time. It is all just matter after all. Just millions of different molecules that for a brief blink of the eye have come together to form a human being.

At any moment, one not of our choosing, they will unform again. They will return to the earth where they can be absorbed back into the great chemical composition. Then, when the time is right they will attach themselves to other molecules and start to form a new thing. Maybe a tree. Maybe a fish. Maybe something in the future that hasn't yet got a name.

Yes, the body just keeps going. It's not dead. If it was how would it be capable of producing all those unique patterns on her skin that I've seen? How would it manage to create all the weird and wonderful things that Flo has turned into during this last month?

In one sense it's been gruesome. The smell has sent me out the room sometimes. Other times I've sat beside her with the impression that she was moving. Or something was moving over her. It was just that her surface was no longer solid. She wasn't a fixed thing anymore. But in another sense what I've seen has brought me peace. It's comforting to know that we're part of something so much greater than ourselves. That no matter what our worries, our mistakes, our real and imagined problems, we will soon just be dust on the wind and nothing can follow us there. Rolled round in earth's diurnal course. Exactly that.

The first thing I noticed was how pale she was. More white than pale. I didn't know she was dead at first. I suspected that she was. But I wasn't certain. She could have just had a stroke. But when I held her wrist to find a pulse there was none. And I left white fingerprints on her skin. This was on the first day. Before I hopped onto the bed and let my legs dangle off it. I know now that this is called Pallor Mortis. It's the first of four post-death stages. It occurs very quickly, within half an hour, and is what happens when the blood stops moving around in us.

She wasn't cold then, but by evening she was. Not completely cold. Cool, rather. I was a little disappointed to tell the truth. When I put my hand on her neck – I was so tempted to squeeze that wart – I was expecting it to be like if you've just had a cold shower or when you come out of the sea. But she wasn't much cooler than room temperature. And when I went back the following morning, after the sun had been on her for a few hours, she was actually warm again. *She's alive! She's alive!* She wasn't. It's a fallacy that dead people just get cold. It's just that they don't warm up from the inside anymore. Like all inanimate things they just reflect the temperature around them. Algor Mortis.

She was set rigid by then. But sat in her chair you'd not

really have noticed. You could only really see the difference in her face. She looked like she was about to say something. Have I said that before? That was the Rigor Mortis. First your muscles go limp, then the bands within them contract. As they would do anyway. But the energy required to expand them again is no longer available, so they stick. It froze her neck and jaw and her half-closed eyelids. Like one of those photographs that catch a person blinking. At some point I closed her eyes properly rather than have her gazing out in that ghoulish, zombie-like way. That's why people used to believe that the eyes retained the last image they looked at. Because of the look frozen onto the face. It's called optography. Some people still believe it's true. It's not.

I have a few other observations from the first few days. The parts of her that were pointing downwards filled with blood. Her earlobes, fingertips, the bottoms of her legs. She was wearing a dress and sandals. This was just plain old gravity doing its thing. Nothing special. At the same time where her arms were pressed on the rest of the chair, her skin was completely white. The contrast was quite remarkable. I've since discovered this was because the blood cells were being squashed and the heart wasn't there to force blood through them. Again, fairly basic stuff.

The next bit, I'm not sure I should say. Flo? Forgive me, Flo. But there's no shame. And she's returned to Doris again now anyway. I didn't notice it at first. I noticed the smell before anything else. It was an unmistakable smell. I lifted up the hem of her dress to make sure and there it was, showing through the white of her underwear. But it's all very natural. It's just because the muscles relax. I'm reminded now of something she told me. I can't believe she did. It's that Derek again. She was there for Christmas. I think it must have been after I'd moved in next door because she was already very old. Anyway, she wet herself while sitting on their new couch. He said it didn't matter, but she heard him talking in the kitchen. She didn't tell me what he said, but afterwards she asked him to bring her home. And he did. He actually did. At Christmas. He dumped her back here in this flat and drove off to enjoy his turkey dinner without her. I wonder when his body will start this grim process. Soon, I hope.

Anyway, all this that happened to her was just preparation for the main event. Just as dying is a process, death sets off another process, and the final part of that is decomposition. It's the most visceral part because it's the part that actually returns us to whence we came. But it's all natural.

The type of decomposition that's happening to Doris Broadbent is called putrefaction. It's the most common kind of decomposition. The others are mummification and adipocere, but the environmental conditions aren't right for them to occur here so I've not even bothered to read what they're about.

Putrefaction is basically the soft tissues of the body turning to liquid in order to seep into the ground and be absorbed. That's not easy when the ground is an insulated floor. Which explains the puddle forming beneath her chair.

It can take a long time, but with Flo it started within a week. I think because of where she was sitting, with the sun blazing on her all day. Green blotches formed on the skin of her arms and hands. That was the first sign. It usually starts in the abdomen because the blotches are where the bacteria is taking over, and our guts are full of bacteria. But I saw it on her hands and arms first. I don't know if it was already on her stomach by then. I didn't look. Every day the patterns on her were different. It was really quite wondrous. Like watching a fern growing beneath her skin.

Less pleasant was the way she swelled up with gas. That was also caused by the bacteria. She puffed right up. Her eyes bulged out and she stuck her tongue out at me. For days on end she kept this up.

'Stop mocking me,' I said. I seriously considered bursting her at one point. I thought I'd be doing us both a favour. She must have been so uncomfortable, all bloated like that. *Poof!* she'd go. Much better. But I resisted. The thought of what would come out of her held me back.

Anyway, that's passed now. We've moved on to the final stage. I said it was like she was moving. That's because she is. Ever so gradually now. Seeping. Not moving. Large swathes of her skin have blistered but they've not crusted over. Like you'd expect. No new skin has been formed. That's allowed the blisters to liquify into a reddish brown fluid that in recent days has started oozing down her body – gravity again – sloughing off what's left of her flesh and taking that down with it too.

As disgusting as it is, you can get absorbed. You can forget you're looking at a former person and focus in on one spot and find yourself getting drawn into the long, slow trickle. Flo by name...

I can't see it because of her clothes, but I know also that every day now more of her insides are turning to mush. It's not just her skin. I wouldn't be surprised if she was at the stage now that I could reach into her belly and pull a handful out. That's where it starts. The intestines and stomach. After that will be the liver, heart, lungs, brain, kidneys, bladder. All the rest of her.

All apart from the tendons and ligaments. They're made of sterner stuff and if we're both still here in six months' time – we won't be, thank God, the Great White Hope will have affected a change of some kind – but if we are, then they'd probably still be clinging to her bones. I'd also be able to see her hair and nails. They don't go anywhere for a while either. But they don't keep growing. That's another falsehood. It just looks like they're growing because the body is shrinking, so as the body disappears the proportion of what's left that is hair and nails increases. Or so I'm led to believe. But that's still to come. That's the future.

I step away from her. I am done. I am finally done. I challenge myself to breathe in deeply but I can't bring myself to do it. I start but then it catches in my throat and I cough and nearly choke. Out the window is the big, beautiful sea. On the other side of it is Germany. Or Belgium. Or the Elysian Fields where Flo and Len are sitting by their window again. I look down at what is there. What would your Len say now? But he's one to talk. The state he must be in. There's her bed. Their bed. Looking at it fills me suddenly with sorrow. *I'm so sorry. I'm so, so sorry. I didn't mean any of it.* I wish they would come for me now. And end all this. For both of us. *You don't deserve this.* There's the kettle and the tray where we put the biscuits that time. The biscuits are still in the cupboard. They will be stale now. The mice can have them. There is the lighter on the table. The table is stained with the rings from a thousand cups. But where is Flo? I walk toward the door. I stop and turn around one last time. There is nothing for me here. She is not here. My friend has gone.

Chapter Nineteen
Then

I am The Pilot. Not the co-pilot. None of that. I'm not playing games now. The Pilot. That's how I've been introduced. *We're delighted to have with us today... We're really grateful that he's taxied into our school this morning... Put your seatbelts on because we're about to hear from...*

The Pilot.

There are sixty-four eyes watching me. Grace's are among them. She's three rows from the back and four from the front. She doesn't know it now but she's watching me with the same eyes that will watch her first child when they're learning to ride a bike. So proud. So proud. So proud. Don't fall.

In many ways I've been looking forward to this morning. I've even done some prep. I'm lying about so many things now, and to so many people, that I'm not even bothered about lying to these innocents. I look at their pure, gullible faces. The teacher steps back to leave the stage to me. She's not the same teacher who asked me to speak to the kids a few weeks ago. She's not as attractive. I might not have said yes to her. No pencil skirts and blouses here. Cords and a frumpy jumper. I'm not even bothered if I impress her or not.

I start talking.

'I've heard people say – unimaginative people, not like us...'
– this is a trick of communication. You include the audience in
your gang and they're already on your side. You give them a
compliment, a good characteristic, and they want to live up to it
– '...that if people were meant to fly then God would've given us
wings. I don't know about that. But what I do know is that he
gave us the vision to want to fly, and the brains to learn how.'

I've always fancied myself as a teacher. I have a natural
affinity with children. Young children. This lot are nine.
They're borderline. They might just sneak under the wire now
but in a year they'd be lost to me.

'I know you've been learning about the Wright brothers.
Orville and Wilbur. Kitty Hawk, South Carolina.' I'm meant to
say the year now but I've forgotten it. 'Can anyone tell me what
year that was?' I ask. This is called thinking on your feet. A boy
shouts out 1903. It sounds about right but I can't be sure. I
glance at the teacher and she's nodding at him. So I nod at him
also.

'Well done. Exactly right. Or Wright. Haha.' They don't
laugh. 'With a W.' Still nothing. I move smoothly on. 'Well,
since the Wright brothers first took flight in 1903, planes have
developed a great deal. They can now travel further and faster
than even Orville and Wilbur would have imagined.

'One of the greatest breakthroughs was moving from
propellers to jet engines. That happened in...' I pause. I looked
this up, too. Nope. It's gone. 'Anyone?' I look at the boy who
answered the first time. He stares blankly back. 'No? Well, it
doesn't really matter when. The main thing to know is that it
was a landmark change in the way planes are powered.'

And so I go on. I'm warming to my theme. Transatlantic
flights. The Concorde. The jumbo jet. A little interlude on time
zones and jet lag. The children are listening. Grace is listening.

She is watching me with big eyes. She is relieved. I could really have been a pilot. I feel like I am one. I should have rented a uniform. I nearly did. I bet the teacher would have approved. I smile at her. She smiles back. Actually, she's not bad. In a motherly sort of way. She's not as old as she's dressed. She might be hiding a tight little body in there. The minx. Landing gear. Safety processes. A reference to 9/11. Globalisation. But in its simplest form. I'm nearly finished.

'But I don't want this to be a history lesson. I'm not going to be testing you on names and dates.' Another subtle us-against-them line. 'Instead, this is about inspiration. It's about having a dream. And believing in it. No matter what anyone else says.' I'm talking exclusively to Grace now. I want her to remember this. 'Just think what people would have thought about those brothers more than 100 years ago. *You want to build a contraption that can fly? With you in it? Are you insane? You'll kill yourself.* But the brothers ignored those people. They believed in themselves. And they did it. History is full of people like the Wright brothers. They invented electricity. They wrote books. They ran faster than anyone said they could. The world we live in today is because of them and what they achieved. And it's a great world. Don't let anyone tell you differently. It really is. It's exciting. It's changing. It's leaving us old folks behind. I'm already asking Grace how the TV works.' Her classmates grin at her. She looks down, blushing. 'It's your world now. But.' Dramatic pause. 'The choice is yours. What you do with it and what role you play in it. You will meet lots of people who will tell you why you can't. Do you want to listen to them? Do you want to be like them? Or do you want to be like the Wright brothers? And fly.'

In my head there is rapturous cheering. Chairs are toppled as they jump to their feet. A few pilgrims even climb on desks. Grace is one of them. Her adoring eyes. I'm a superhero when

I'm with her. *Oh captain, my captain.* I swallow hard. Get a grip. There is a touch on my shoulder. The teacher is there. She is looking at the class, telling them to thank me for my time. I put my hand up. No. Really. It was my pleasure. Grateful for the opportunity. I am about to depart. The teacher's hand is still on my shoulder though. She's not letting me go.

'Have you got time for a few questions?'

I hadn't planned on this. I thought it would just be turning up and saying my thing. I rush through the scenarios. None of them turn out terribly. I decide I can wing it.

'Yes. Sure. No worries.'

It starts off well enough. Have I seen a UFO? No. How high do we usually fly? About 35,000 feet. I remember this from holidays abroad. Too easy. What's the scariest thing that's happened to me in a cockpit? I talk at length about a near mid-air collision. Over Birmingham. It was many years ago and my plane and the other one were not that close, really. About 1,000 yards. But when you're flying at that speed, 'not that close' can feel too close for comfort.

'Safety is always our number one concern,' I say earnestly. 'A pilot's first responsibility is always to the passengers. To get them down safely.'

I believe it myself. I'm so convincing. When did I learn to lie like this? Where does it all come from? It's got to be a talent. Not everyone can do it. It just comes naturally to me. There's not even a difference anymore. Between a truth and an untruth. All these faces watching me. Believing me. And Grace's among them. I don't look at her. I wish she wasn't here now.

Do I eat the same food as the passengers? Haha. Would they get sucked out if they broke the window? How long does it take to learn to be a pilot? A long time. How long? Long. How long did it take you? Ages. The boy who knew the year of the Wright brothers hasn't raised his hand. Good. I don't want him to. I've gone off him. I look at the teacher. I'm ready to go.

'Okay,' she says, 'we've only got time for a few more questions.'

A few more? Jesus. Okay. I can manage that. Have I ever hit a bird? Lots of times. Usually it's quite safe. What about lightning? Um. I talk about radar helping us to avoid storms. Deflection. Another trick. I don't like the way the Wright brothers boy is staring at me. I have no idea about lightning strikes. It must happen all the time. It can't bring a plane down or I'd have read about it. The radar keeps us well clear of thunderstorms most of the time, I say again. What's it like flying through clouds? Can computers land planes by themselves? Enough now. I'm done. Let's not get cocky. I look at the teacher but she's looking at the Wright brothers boy, who has raised his hand now.

'Okay, last question. James?'

'How fast do you need to be going to take off?'

It could have been worse. A real curveball. But that's pretty straightforward. I should be okay. Only I don't know the answer. Every pilot would know the answer without thinking. I remember the times I've sat in a plane at take-off. I can feel the force pushing me back in the seat. I can see the tarmac, blue out the window. On wet days moisture streams backwards across the glass. What speed do you need to reach to make that happen? I tell the boy that I'm glad he asked that. That it's a good question.

'Here's an interesting fact about speed,' I say. I've decided not to answer his question, but to answer a similar one instead. 'Did you know the speed aircraft travel through the air isn't always the same as the speed they travel over the ground? Anyone know why?' But I don't give them the chance to answer. I want to answer this. I want them to know that I know. This is my wild card. 'Wind. It's quite simple. If a plane has a headwind – that means if it's flying into the wind – its airspeed will be greater than its ground speed because it has to make up for the force of the wind. And the opposite is true for a tail-wind.' I smile at Wright brothers. 'You can impress your friends with that fact.'

'But what about taking off?' he asks. The little shit.

'Oh, well, that all depends on a number of factors. Lots of different things. Okay?' It's not okay. He's still waiting. I look at the teacher. She smiles back at me. She's waiting too. I decide she's ugly, after all. 'Things like the weather. The load. The weight of the plane. What type of aircraft it is. Lots of things. It's quite complicated, really.'

'What about a full 747?' he says. 'Or a full 707? Or a small plane?'

'Exactly right,' I say. I look at my feet. I notice they have turned a little towards the door. I didn't know liars did that with their feet, but apparently it's a scientific fact. If you want to know if someone is lying, see if their feet are pointing at the exit. They want out. I want out now too. I should just make up a number. But I've not got the faintest clue. Fast. Is fast a number?

'He doesn't even know.'

'James!'

'He doesn't though, Miss. He didn't know about lightning either.'

'James, I'm not telling you again!'

'I bet he's not even a real pilot.'

I'm waiting for Grace at the school gates. Normally I'd meet her in the playground but she asked me to wait here instead today. I'm looking out for the mums. The sun is out. They might be dressed down. Ah. Here she comes. Grace sees me but looks away quickly. She raises a hand in greeting. Did she? Or did she just hike up her schoolbag. It was the same gesture.

'Hello,' I say, as she gets nearer. She mumbles something at my feet but doesn't stop walking. I spot one of the mums. The redhead. The Dolores lookalike. No. Not today. The hair is wrong. No sign of the other one. I turn to leave. Grace has not waited for me. She's twenty yards away already. I walk quickly to catch up to her. Big, adult strides. By the time I'm alongside her again we're almost at the corner. She's still not looked at me. As we turn I look back towards the gate. There is James. Walking out of it. With someone I assume to be his brother. His shirt is untucked. James's shirt, I mean. And he's dragging his schoolbag along the gutter with one hand. He's scum. I bet his family is scum too. I loathe them all. Even the grandmother in the home and the aunt on dialysis. Draining the resources of the world.

'I didn't think it went too badly,' I say. I don't say that it didn't go too badly considering the night I had. Just the thought of it recalls the smell of stale wine and sick. A small spurt of aftertaste shoots into the back of my throat and I swallow it back down. I wonder what her mother will say to me. Once the dust has settled. She wasn't happy. Whenever she calls me Adrian I know. 'The last part was a bit awkward. Who was that boy? The know-it-all? What a loser! But the rest was okay. The stuff about imagination, and about the jets. And the way I ended it, when I said about it being your world now, that was pretty good, I thought. No? You don't agree?'

She slows down. I slow down. She speeds up. I speed up. I am trying to think what else I can say to her. I can't think of anything. It doesn't feel right to go for ice cream today. 'Did you have a good sleepover?' No answer. 'Can I take your bag?' She drops it off her shoulder onto the ground and keeps on walking.

I have to stop to pick it up. My back aches when I bend down now. I put my hand on it and pull a face. When I stand up again I see that Grace has stopped now and is staring at me. I smile. But then I stop smiling.

'A plane has to go 150 miles an hour to take off,' she says. 'Any idiot could look that up. And James is my friend!'

I watch her run away down the road. Her grey school skirt swishes around her legs. I take my phone out. I want to check. Because 150 miles per hour doesn't seem fast enough. She's right though. Between 150 and 180mph. And while I'm at it... let's see... no, lightning strikes rarely bring down planes. They have systems to discharge the energy safely, leaving little or no evidence. Clever. Clever but not wise. I look up. Grace is nearly at our turning. She's running slower, but still running. I watch her until she disappears behind the wall on the corner.

Chapter Twenty
Then

Dolores sees me come in. She is waiting. She has turned on the light and sat down at the table to wait. She must have wondered what was taking me so long. We've not spoken about it yet. My revelation of last night. All day we've deliberately not spoken about it.

'I've made you breakfast,' she said this morning. Not to me. She beamed at Grace when she said it. She never did that. Breakfast or beamed. 'Daddy didn't want any,' she added, although Grace hadn't asked. When we were getting our coats on she made a point of coming into the hallway to kiss her goodbye and wish her luck for the day.

'Keep the flag flying,' she said.

'What?' said Grace. 'Okay. I'll try.' I looked at her confused face. She didn't know about any flag. What flag? So how was she expected to keep it flying? She started to tell her mother about the talk I'd be giving to her class, but stopped just in time. She looked at me, proud as punch that she'd remembered. I winked at her. She didn't know that I'd spilled the beans already. And other vegetables. That she could've said anything at all and not made it any worse. I turned around at the end of the path.

Dolores was in the doorway. She was watching us, but blankly, her thoughts had already taken her somewhere else.

'Go and give your mother another kiss,' I said. Grace ran up to her and wrapped her arms around her waist. Dolores picked her up and held her. She closed her eyes and put her head close to her daughter's. She said something in her ear. I saw Grace nod. Dolores put her down again and waved the whole time we were walking away. Not once did she look at me. Not directly. I half expected her to not come home tonight. But she did. She was back before us. With the same brittle cheerfulness as before. I've matched it with my own and together we have spent the evening filling the house with how cheerful we both are.

'Are you and Mummy arguing?'

We adults think we're so clever. But we're kidding ourselves if we think we can kid our children.

'Of course not!'

'No, dear.'

'Young imaginations. Hahaha.'

'It's just that you've not looked at each other. Or said anything to each other.'

But now it is evening. Now Grace is in bed. And Dolores is ready. She has things she wants to say. I knew it was coming. That's why I lingered in the garden. When I took the bins out. I stopped under the tree and ran the outside of my foot along the ground. It had rained and the earth was soft. I made a shallow furrow in the soil without even pressing hard. I was planning my defence. I'd seen the light go on and knew she'd be there when I returned. Good. It will be good to have it out. To clear the air. We'll talk about my job. Obviously. My job will be the words we'll use.

But really we'll be talking about something else. I thought I'd start by telling her that we are all living things. That we are alive. I couldn't possibly be expected to grow and flourish in such a stifling atmosphere. I needed natural light. My desk was the furthest from the window. And space. We all need space. Some more than others. I'd remind her softly that I'd tried talking to her about this but she'd not taken me seriously. So really, what did she expect? Surely she couldn't have expected me to suffer in silence forever. I'd tell her also that I was pleased for her. That she got so much from her job. So much what? Stimulation and excitement. I'd say it so it didn't sound like a petty innuendo. I'd ask her to try to understand and appreciate how lucky she was, but not everyone was as fortunate. That I was a living thing. Could I repeat that line? I thought I could. For emphasis. And that I was withering and dying there. I had to act. I'd admit I didn't know what I was doing now. Or next. But that whatever was coming had to be better than whatever had been. And it would be. With her support. We could make it so. Union reformed.

'Are you kicking me out?'

That is what I actually say. When I sit down opposite her. The mud on my shoe has left muck on the tiles. I see her looking at it.

'I've not decided yet.'

'Because of the job situation.'

'Among other things.'

Other things. I don't ask. I don't want to know. There are three footprints on the floor. Between me and the back door. They are all from my right foot. The one I scraped in the soil.

'Grace then, if you're too afraid to ask. I hate what you're doing to her. I wasn't going to say anything. But it seems the right time now. Cards on the table.'

'Grace? What do you mean?'

'Oh please. It's clear as day. How you're pitting her against me. Turning me into the mean old mum. Making her pick. No. Don't interrupt. I will finish. I don't say this with any malice.

But I want to warn you. Because I know you love her and she adores you. And I care for you both. But it will backfire. I promise you. You can't keep her for yourself. One day something will happen, you'll say something or she'll remember something, and suddenly everything will become clear to her. She's young now. But she won't always be young.'

Dolores should be a barrister. No defendant would stand a chance. I have taken the time to consider and plan my defence. But she has completely broadsided me. How could I have predicted this line of attack? I want to say that I can't help it if I am her favourite. That if she prefers being with me that is maybe because I am more attentive. Perhaps if she wasn't at work all the time. Or didn't have her head in her phone when she wasn't. Something stops me. I say nothing.

'That's the first thing,' Dolores continues. 'That's all I'm saying about it. Just think about it. It's your bed to lie in otherwise. Right. The job situation. As you call it.' She crosses her arms and sits back in her chair. She has a twitch. When she is nervous. Or tense. It is a little pulse in her neck. Hardly visible. It usually only comes when she is worried about work. It is there now. She rubs it absently. I have a powerful urge to get up and hold this woman. I suppress it.

'What have you been doing all this time? During the day, I mean.'

'Nothing really.'

'Is that it? Hardly Churchill, is it? I'm giving you a chance here.'

'Okay. Well, this morning I took Grace to school. I gave that talk to her class—'

'What talk?'

'Just something her teacher mentioned to me a few weeks ago.'

'What talk?'

'About being the best version of yourself.' I hear how that must sound to her. I wait. Nothing. She only thinks her comeback. I continue. 'Then I went out into the country. To look for Reggie again. I got some sunshine on my face. I enjoyed some recreational drug use. Because I'm a grown-up and I can do what I want. I enjoyed that. Then I came home. Fetched Grace. Helped her with her homework. Took the bins out. And now here I am.'

'And yesterday? And the day before?'

'Much the same. Apart from the talk.'

I listen for sounds outside the room. I want to make sure Grace hasn't woken up and crept to the other side of the door. I know how children can be affected when their parents argue. It threatens them. Undermines their security. But there is nothing. Not a creaking stair or sighing floorboard.

'What's wrong with you?'

'Nothing.'

'If you believe that, that's even more worrying.'

'Why should something be wrong? Just because I resigned? People do it every day.'

'You didn't resign. You quit. You walked out. I checked. It's different. And then you lied to me about it.'

'I didn't lie.'

'Not telling is the same as lying.'

'I told you yesterday.'

'You embarrassed me.'

'Because I told you in front of Joe? You're always in front of Joe.'

She stops herself saying what she was about to say. She breathes in slowly through her nose then exhales through her mouth. Her cheeks are red though. Either she is angry or she's been exposed.

'Secondly, you're taking drugs again. All the time. And

around your child. Our child. That's unforgivable. If there was nothing else, that alone is unforgivable. And what else? Oh. You've lost our dog. You've actually lost him. You loved him. What happened to him? He wouldn't have just run off. And then you sit there and say nothing is wrong? Adrian?'

My name again. In full. I hate when she says it in that tone. It makes me feel like a little boy she is admonishing.

'Well, when you put it like that.'

'I'm not putting it like anything. These are just the facts. You know, I was warned against marrying you. They said I needed someone who wanted to change the world and you'd only want to change the channel. Please don't smirk like that. You know what I said? I said I didn't care. That you had already changed *my* world. Can you imagine it? Can you imagine me saying something like that?'

I can't. And I don't believe she did. But she is clever like that. Making a point I can neither prove nor disprove.

'I knew it was a gamble. I knew you could go either way. But I honestly thought you'd latch on to something. That something would inspire you and you'd become... almost great. You had it in you.' Past tense. I notice that. 'It's not going to happen, is it? Instead, you have... you have...'

I see her head turn to the side. She is thinking of a word. I can hear her mind trying out the alternatives. I try to predict which one she'll choose. *Changed.* That will be it.

'Shrunk,' she says.

Shrunk. Smaller than what was before. Less than. Something that has become a reduced version of itself. I don't have a dictionary to hand but that is the general meaning. The barrister in her again. Choosing just the right word for maximum effect. Shrunk. It makes sense from where she is sitting. I can see that. I certainly occupy less space in her thoughts. But she is wrong. I've only shrunk from her. From the version of myself she thought she was marrying, or wanted to coax out of me. The go-getter. Suits and salaries. I was never him. If she thought I was then the fault was hers. I think of Grace upstairs, tucked up snug and warm in her bed. Dreaming her little girl fairy-tale dreams. Chantal. That was her name. The Queen. I've created a whole world for her. She is their favourite human. And I am hers. I've not shrunk in her eyes.

'Grace appreciates me,' I say.

She looks away. At the mud on the floor. 'You have shrunk. You have. That's why you cling to Grace. She's the only one left who's your size. The adults have outgrown you.'

'Are you sleeping with him, Dee?'

'Excuse me?'

'You heard.'

'Jesus. The shit in your head.'

'That's not an answer.'

'We're done here,' she says. She stands up.

'Yes or no, Dee?'

She starts walking away. I remain where I am, staring at my hands on the table. I listen to her shoes on the tiles. They make a different sound when she reaches the carpet. Softer. But still audible. She is getting away.

'Yes or no?' I shout after her. But it's rhetorical. She won't answer me and I don't really care either way. If I had to guess I'd say that she probably is sleeping with Joe, and that I can't blame her. She can't help what she wants, and I can't help not being it. I think we've resigned ourselves to this situation. After years of rubbing together like two uneven surfaces. Her urging me to do something. Something big or small. Me sulking until she stops nagging. All that's left of that friction now is a tut or a roll of the eyes. There is little left to get worked up about. The surface is smooth. What she said about me and Grace. It is all true. It's my revenge. I've known for years. Only I've never framed it quite so clearly. Hearing her say it all so simply makes it true and unavoidable. I look up. She is in the doorway. I didn't hear her come back.

'Yes,' she says.

Yes what? It takes me a moment.

Chapter Twenty-One
Then

Grace is sitting cross-legged on the floor. She is surrounded by dolls. She has fourteen of them. By my reckoning that is about fourteen too many. I'm out of my comfort zone here. But I try my best. I know all their names. I don't know which name goes with which doll. But I've got fourteen names.

There is Chloe. I know her because she was the first. She's been here the longest. I remember choosing her. There is Jessica. Daisy. Deborah. Debbie. Wait. Are Deborah and Debbie the same one? Becki. With an i. The new way. Trendy. Trendy with a y. The right way. Erica. Zoe. Ah, Zoe. I linger a little guiltily over her. If any of these dolls were real I'd want it to be Zoe. Long blonde hair. Enormous blue eyes. A body out of proportion in the most pneumatic way. I'd happily come upstairs and play with her in the afternoons. Katy. Lisa. Bethany. Rachel... I'm struggling now. How many is that? Eleven. Eleven or twelve. Depending on the Debbie verdict. The others. They will come to me.

I'm not comfortable down here. Sitting on the floor. It's beginning to tell on my joints. What I'm doing is undressing the doll and then putting it into a new outfit. That's what Grace was doing when I came in, uninvited – but after knocking, I always knock now, she's of an age – so that's what I'm doing. But what I'm really doing is studying her for any tiny tell. I'm trying to decide if she's upset generally or upset with me. Because she's not said a word since I collected her from school.

She brushed right past me. At the school gate. Not a hello. Not even a frown to let me know she was angry with me. She brushed past me like I wasn't there. She's nine. She's at that awkward age. I try not take these things too personally. I wondered at first if it was still about my talk. The fallout from that. I imagine her friends could have been a little mean about it if they'd chosen to. I fear my mask is slipping. My superhero one. She's learning, inevitably, that we're all just people. Even us daddies. We're just ordinary people. One of millions. Billions. Eight billion in fact. We can't pretend for ever. She went straight upstairs. When we got home.

'Did you want something to eat?' I called to her back. She didn't stop. I left her alone then. I didn't want to press. I can't help but notice how much uglier she is when she's angry. I've noticed before. I hate seeing it. Her face becomes pinched. The too-small features all crowd together. They take up even less of her face. I listened to her banging around upstairs. In her room first. Then in our room. Then in her room again. I waited a little longer then I went into the garden. It's L-shaped so I can go around the corner and not be seen through any of the windows. Even the upstairs ones. I am getting too used to it now. My vice of choice. I watched the smoke waft up white into the green leaves but I felt next to nothing. I'm getting nothing from it anymore. I'll stop again soon. Binge over. Then I'll regroup and come back better than ever. Ready to grasp whatever opportunities present themselves. I came back inside and decided to have a lie down. That's when I found the letters. They were on my bed. Or our bed. I knew what they were as soon as I saw them. I didn't even have to open them.

So I don't think it was my talk that's upset her. That has stilled her tongue. That's why I'm studying her secretly. The way she picks the dolls up. Pulls their arms into sleeves. Puts them down again. Our bodies talk all the time. They say what we're really feeling.

Half the dolls are naked now. They are in a mass grave on her right. The other half are dressed again. They're sitting in a long upright row on her left. Sophie. That's another one. And Olivia. Is there one more? I want to say Emma. In front of her is the pile of their miniature clothes and shoes.

I don't know the name of the doll I'm now holding. I know it's not Zoe. I am trying to fit her into a blue dress. She has those plastic arms that don't bend and fingers that seem to catch on everything. I can't get the dress on. I have put her hands up above her head, in front of her, straight down by her side. Each way I try it the dress gets stuck. There must be a knack I don't have. A trick I don't know about. I wonder if Dolores knows it. I bet if we had sons there'd be things I could do, would just instinctively know, that she'd have no clue about. The way to line up our soldiers, with the flag on high ground behind the front line. The way you can't just die when you get shot. You have to do it in slow motion, pull faces, make noises, slide down the wall. She'd get it wrong. I hold the doll, whoever she is, in front of me and consider the angles. I will get her into this blasted blue dress even if I have to rip it. Perhaps if I – Grace snatches it out of my hands and slaps her down on the pile of naked bodies. It's not Emma. It's Eva. The last one. Strange name for a doll.

'Sorry,' I say.

I think of what I should say next and then think it's best to say nothing. Then she will talk first and I'll discover what it is

I'm sorry about. This is my special parenting trick. Doing nothing. Parents always get this part wrong. They say too much. And too often. It's much more effective to listen more and speak less. Especially at the key moments. I sit back on my hands. Yes, I'm too old to be down here. My joints are aching. They're not meant to open up like this. And especially not for this length of time. It's my hips mainly. But my knees and ankles too. I try to arch my back. To stretch it out. You can't do it when you're sitting like this. It just makes other parts hurt more.

She is still saying nothing. She doesn't look like she's about to. I keep waiting.

One thing that's always struck me about her room is how light it is. No matter what the time of day. It's because it's at the top of the house so manages to have a window on each side. That means the sun can always get in no matter where it is in the sky. As a toddler she'd sit beneath whichever window had the sun and play for hours by herself. I see her fine hair stuck to her head in the sticky heat of the loft. The whole image seems so unreal now. More like a scene that would be drawn into a children's book than real life. But it was real. I watched her for hours. So self-contained. So lost to herself. It was a marvel. I didn't think there was another two-year-old in the world who could have been so silent for so long. She's made up for lost time now though.

I realise she's not going to speak. I could sit here all day. She's stubborn. Like her mother. Like me? Like us both probably. In some ways. But the mix means she's also nothing like us. A completely new thing. A marvel. As I say. Okay. I can't wait all day. I decide if we're going to get anywhere then it's up to me to generate the action. I reach into my pocket and pull out the letters. I just hold them for a moment in my lap. Now I'm really studying her. She's not surprised to see them. Why should she be? She put them there for me to find. She's been waiting for me to give them back to her. I put them down on the carpet between us.

'I found these. On our bed. Did you want them back?'

She still won't talk. The doll she has in her hands has short hair. I realise how odd that is. Almost unheard of. From a distant past I seem to recall us cutting her hair. Or Grace showing me after she'd cut it. Bethany. I am sure that's her name. Bethany with the bob. That's how I remembered it. I pick up the letters and put them down again.

'I'll leave them here then, shall I?'

I'm getting nothing from her. It's quite remarkable how she's able to hide from me whatever she's thinking. I'm impressed. But also a little worried. It's not healthy. I decide enough is enough. I make to get up.

'I don't want them,' she says. I sit back down again. Almost reluctantly. I've got pins and needles. I could cramp at any moment.

'Oh. Okay. That's fine.'

I pick up the letters and lean right over to my side to push them down into my pocket. Out of sight. Instinctively I think it's important they're not seen anymore. The effort makes me grunt. I don't mean to. I'm getting old. I'll be walking about with my hands behind my back soon, sighing when I get in and out of chairs. Grace will have a family of her own. I'll only be on the edge of it. Where does the time go?

'Can I ask why?'

She was GeeGee on the grass. She was Gracie with her arms outstretched beneath the blossom tree that May morning, and Miss Graceful on the first day of school. She is Grace now. Too old for dolls. The next stage is ready to steal her away. She puts Bethany down and picks up another doll. I have no idea who it is. She fiddles among the pile of clothes in front of her but she's not concentrating. In a few moments she has forgotten entirely what she's doing and one by one the different parts of her body stop moving until she is just sitting there, holding the doll, staring at it, absolutely still.

'They're not even real,' she says.

I think she means the dolls. 'It's just playing,' I say stupidly.

She points to my pocket, where the letters are.

'I'm not a baby. I've known for ages. So you can stop writing them now. You can stop lying about it.'

She begins to twist the arm of the doll. The plastic goes white where it bends. She keeps twisting until it refuses to twist any further. Plastic is a marvel too. So durable. It won't break for her. It resists. She gets frustrated and throws the doll down. She picks up a different one. This one has hinges. Her legs bend at the knees. Grace grabs it around the waist and with her other hand begins to push the foot the wrong way. The leg straightens but it won't go back anymore. I look at Grace's contorted face. Devastatingly, heart-breakingly ugly. She is pushing as hard as she can. Her teeth are clenched. She's glaring at it. I don't think she's even breathing. I watch her face get redder and redder. The leg doesn't move. Grace leans right over it, pushing her whole weight against it. She presses down, down, down. Suddenly the hinge breaks and the leg snaps off completely. Grace's hand shoots down and punches the floor. I wince at the impact but she doesn't. She looks at the leg. There is blood on the plastic. It's from her knuckles. Where they hit the carpet. She licks where she is bleeding and then watches. Nothing happens for a moment. Then more blood forms on the surface. Like a spring. She puts her knuckle in her mouth.

'I wasn't really lying,' I say. I'm not sure it's the right thing. But I'm confused. She said she's known for ages. About the letters. So why is she upset now? 'Is that what's upset you?'

She looks up at me under hooded eyes. The look in them. The disgust. I almost don't know this person. Sometimes the woman she'll one day be comes out. She does now and shocks me. The ugliness of her. It's not her face. Not just her face. It's the hardness that's set in because of her appearance. Because of the pain it's caused her. The hardness and the distrust. Time won't heal her. I feel my heart give way. I love her so much. I only wanted the magic to last. That's why I wrote them. How do I say that? Dolores would know. I lean forward. I'm smiling gently. I want to hold her. But she pulls away sharply.

'You told Mummy.' Her bottom lip trembles and she bites it hard. 'It was our secret. You promised.'

Chapter Twenty-Two
Then

I don't have to go on the rampage. I really don't. That's the God's honest truth. It is a conscious decision. I start at a moment of my choosing and I can cease at any moment too. I am in complete control. I am at all times aware of what I am breaking, and how I am breaking it.

There is an old vase. It doesn't get any older. There is a cabinet full of plates and other crockery that we never use. It makes an awful noise when it hits the floor. Some of the plates push the glass doors open while the cabinet is still tottering on its edge. They slip off their shelves and jump to their deaths rather than allowing themselves to be crushed. There is a laptop. It is still plugged in. Its screen shows a tropical waterfall. It takes a handful of attempts to finally shatter it. Hardy things. Deceptively robust. There is a wooden ornament, not much taller than a mug but very heavy, mahogany maybe. It makes a very neat hole in the window. This is after the curtains have been ripped off their rails.

I am enjoying myself now. There seems to be an endless amount of potential for destruction in our house. I hadn't realised how much stuff we've accumulated. Too much. Where did that stone turtle come from? Who in their right mind thought we'd want it in our home? And yet there it is. On the windowsill. Until it is no longer on the windowsill. But flying through another window and landing on the lawn. And this lamp? And this picture? And this chair? Why is it in the hallway? Whoever sits on it? Look at that. Look at how its legs just snap off. I think of a stupid but not stupid line I've read somewhere – either we own our possessions or our possessions own us. Is it the Buddhists who urge us to give up all our possessions, or do they say just that we should take no pleasure in them? I am doing both. I am giving them up, and I am certainly not allowing them to give me pleasure.

Dolores is here in the centre of it. The storm rages around her but doesn't touch her. She follows me from room to room. Occasionally she speaks to me. *Please,* she says, or *not that.* I hear everything she says but I pretend not to. I am pretending that the red mist has come down. That I am lost to reason. Sometimes I make faces. When I pass somewhere I know there is a mirror. I want to see if I look as deranged as I am acting. I don't though. I still look, to me, like the same ineffective, slightly dull man I always have been.

'You think you can take Grace from me?'

I say this a few times. It adds to the drama. I think it creates greater tension. It is all happening a lot quicker than I expect. It doesn't take much time. To break things. To push them over. To throw them somewhere. I think about how much longer it will take to clean all this up. That stops me for a moment. I am standing in the bathroom. Something is in my hand. I look down. It is that wooden ornament again. I thought I'd thrown it out the window. But there it is in physical form. Yet I can see myself in the other room, my arm extended in front of me, watching it fly through the air. Odd. Yes, I pause now and consider all this mess. Perhaps we'll need a skip. Or we can hire professionals. That would be the solution. We could go out for the day and come back to a clean, nearly empty house. And start all over again. I lift up my hand and begin smashing the side of the bath with the ornament. At first my hand just bounces back up again. It is like the bath fighting back. It actually hurts my wrist. The jarring. I'll admit it, this does annoy me. I do get a little angry now. But the bath doesn't resist for long. Not when I begin to hit it with even greater force. With all my force. I am screaming at it while doing it too. Again, just for effect.

Where shall I go now? I don't suppose I need to itemise everything. And provide a chronology. I go from room to room. I leave nothing untouched. I am like a tornado but instead of doing all the damage at once I do it piece by piece. Apart from in Grace's room. I don't go in there. She is in there. The door is closed.

She was with us when I started this. After she'd said about it being our secret, that I'd promised not to tell anyone. She followed me out of her room. She must have known something was going to happen. Maybe I got the look on my face just right then. I don't know. But something warned her. She was at my heels as I rushed around the house. I wasn't breaking things yet. I was looking for Dolores. And then I found her.

'You told her?' I said, meaning Grace. 'About the letters? Why would you do that?'

To be fair to Dolores, she did look contrite at that point. Perhaps she realised she'd done wrong. I'd done wrong too. I accept that. I was about to say that what I'd done wrong was of greater value and brought greater consequences. But I don't believe that. I don't. What can matter more than the trust a daughter has in her father? It's even bigger than trust though. Dolores doesn't understand that. She never will.

'How could you?' I said. 'Not just to me. But to her.'

'The truth hurts,' she said.

It was a remarkably cavalier answer, and didn't begin to address the seriousness of the issue. She shrugged. She had started shrugging a lot. It annoyed me. It was like I was an insect on her shoulder that she couldn't even be bothered to swat away. A twitch would do.

'But.' But what? I couldn't think what to say. I was too flustered to make an argument. To articulate my point. I always lose our arguments anyway. I get emotional. She remains clear-headed. Deliberate. 'But it's so cruel.'

That was all I managed. It wasn't enough. I could see by her face, how little it changed, that it wasn't enough. That's when I decided to break things. I hadn't intended to break as much as I did. Her dressing table was there and I swept everything off it. I looked at Dolores again. Still her face didn't change. I picked a frame off the wall and threw it to the ground. I opened our cupboard and began throwing our clothes on the floor. This I realised early on was futile. They didn't break. Or shatter. Or even make a noise. They just crumpled. But if I stopped halfway I'd have lost face. It was only when I picked up her bedside table and hurled it against the wall that she stopped looking quite so disinterested. That's also when Grace ran away. The bedside table is what really started it. I was just playing up until that point. But that was extreme. It made a statement. It spoke in a way I couldn't. I looked at it on the floor, buckled, splintered, spilling out creams and old cards and all manner of women's secrets. I decided I had more to say.

'I won't come in,' I shout to Grace's door, every time I pass it. 'Don't worry. Daddy loves you.'

I am sweating now. It is finally finished. My hand is bleeding. There is a red smear on my trousers. Near the pocket. There is still more stuff left. I could go on. But I decide enough is enough. I sit down on the couch. Dolores comes in. She looks scared.

Alan Feldberg

'Tea?' I ask her. Tea always calms the nerves. I think it would do her good. I get up and go into the kitchen, then come back. 'Kettle's broken,' I say with a grin. 'We could all go out?'

She walks out of the room again. I don't follow. I hear her knocking on Grace's door. There is no answer.

'Grace, honey? It's Mummy. Daddy's in the other room. Can I come in?'

I wait. She won't let her in. She is still mine. I hear the door open, soft voices, sniffing, then it gently closes again. I heard the click of the lock.

Chapter Twenty-Three
Then

I don't know exactly what Dolores told her about the letters. I don't know how Grace knew. I'll never know. I wasn't there when it happened, and neither of them have told me. But knowing each party as I do, and my relationship with them, I imagine it went something like this:

Dolores is furious at me. About the job. About embarrassing her in front of Joe. About being me. She wants to hurt me. The best way she knows how is through Grace. She finds Grace in her room.

'I need to talk to you. Seriously. I think you're old enough. I want you to know I'm not trying to hurt you. I'm trying to protect you. And you're getting to that age now. You need to know that men can't always be believed. Not all men. Sometimes they tell lies. Not all the lies they tell will affect you. Some of them will. And some of them will hurt you very much. If you let them. I'm telling you this because some of the most painful lies will come from the men you love the most. Who you believe the most. Those who you wouldn't expect to tell you lies. But they know this. That's why they think they can get away with it. And that's why you need to be careful.'

'You mean men like Daddy?'

'Yes.'

'Okay. But Daddy wouldn't lie to me.'

'He might do.'

'He wouldn't.'

'He might. He lies to me.'

Grace would know this was true because of what happened about my job.

'Your father lies to everyone.'

Grace would know that was true, also, after my little talk at her school. But she'd be 100 per cent certain that I wouldn't lie to her. Not about important things. She might accept that I've probably told her a few falsehoods. Like that her eyes would go square if she watched too much TV, or she'd get boils if she didn't eat her vegetables, or that I turned down the opportunity to join the boy band she likes – she knew that wasn't true, but she liked me saying it. It had made her laugh. But when it came to important things, she knew I'd not lie to her.

'Not to me,' she'd say again. Defiant.

Her mother would shake her head sadly. But inside she'd be excited. This was the cue she had been waiting for, the chance to finally strip me of my superhero status for the last person on earth who still saw me like that. I wonder if she'd have savoured the moment. Let it linger. Drawn it out. Made more small talk. Or if she'd have been too impatient to apply the coup de grâce.

'I'm sorry, honey, but he does lie to you. Who do you think writes those fairy letters? He's been making a fool of you.'

Chapter Twenty-Four
Then

In the end everything I need fits in a single bag. I don't even fill it. It is on the passenger seat of the car. We have two cars. I am taking the older one. Things in it keep breaking. Costing us more money we don't have. I close the door and stand against the car. It is a beautiful morning. There is a bit of blue sky and a bit of grey. It all looks perfectly normal. I don't think this can be it. I expect something more. I don't know what exactly. Something like the end of a film that lets everyone know it's the end. I go back into the house. Grace is in her room. She is sitting with her back to me.

'Grace? Can I have a hug goodbye.'

She doesn't turn around. I walk in and hug her from behind. She doesn't turn around. She doesn't hug me back. She sits perfectly still. Holding the doll with the broken leg. I close my eyes. I smell her hair. I kiss her on the head. She doesn't turn around. She sits perfectly still.

Dolores is waiting in the hallway. There is no reason for her being there other than to see me off.

'I'm sorry I disappointed you,' I say.

She blinks. It is a long blink. Her eyes are closed a long time.

I think they will be wet when she opens them again. I hope they will. But they aren't. She reaches for the door handle. The door opens.

'Okay,' I say.

I walk out and before I have a chance to turn around I hear the door close behind me. She doesn't slam it. It is soft. The click. Like the door only just reaches the latch. I walk down the path and get in the car. I hope it won't start. Sometimes it doesn't. Sometimes you just have to get out and leave it and try it again the next morning. There is no rhyme or reason to it. I put the key in the ignition. None of this is real. The door will open. They'll come running out. The car does start. I see my hand put it into gear and then I hear the tyres start rolling over the gravel. Very slowly. Hardly moving at all. I can identify every separate crunch. I lean over and look out the passenger window. Grace is at her window. She might be there. I think she is. That shadow. Then the hedge blocks her out and I am looking at the front of someone else's house.

Chapter Twenty-Five
Now

What day is it now? I normally know the number without thinking. I wake up knowing it. But I've lost track. I have a rough idea. It's somewhere between 1,880 and 1,885. But I can't be exact. I'm not sure how long I've been sat in this chair.

Who'd have thought it? Five years. Five whole years. And change. Not me, that's for sure. I never expected this. When I left. I don't know what I expected, but not this. I was sure something would happen. There I go. Walking down the path. Is that even a spring in my step? A hint of one, at least? If it is it's because something was bound to happen. To bring us all back together. I was so certain of it. And of myself. There I am, getting in the car. Look at my hand on the gear stick. I didn't pause. Look at my foot moving from one pedal to the other. There are no consequences. That's what my foot is saying there. There is the car, edging slowly down the road. I'll be back. Or you'll follow me. Something will happen. I don't know what. I don't need to worry about it. Something always happens. I just have to wait. Are there no misgivings? No tears, perhaps? No doubt at all? Of course there are, as I'm driving away. Not the tears. But I'm upset. It's upsetting to be walking out on my family. Even if I was pushed. I'm unsettled because events have overtaken me. They've taken on a life-force all their own. But I'm slightly giddy, too. *Be honest with yourself. Look at your elbow out the window. The way your thumb is tap tapping with nervous energy. You're excited. All your belongings are on the seat beside you. All your future is in front of you.* I'm back there now. I'm watching this naive version of myself driving away. I'm in the back seat.

I can see his face in the rear-view mirror. He has no idea I'm here. That's why there is a smirk on his face. I see it. He thinks he's got it all ahead of him. If you asked him he'd tell you about the Aborigines, about instinct. He'd say something about a kernel being back in his belly telling him he's doing the right thing. What would I say back? I could try to tell him what he's driving towards. I could explain about the emptiness of time, and about how regret manifests itself in the most unusual ways. I could tell him about Flo and about decomposition. I could go on. But he'd not listen. He'd not believe it. Grace is still there with him. That's why he's not worried. He's not left her yet. That was her at the window. But the separation hasn't begun. Not properly. He's still got strands of her hair on his jacket. The sweet wrapper she gave him in the park – *I've got a present for you, close your eyes and hold out your hand* – is still in his back pocket. There is her hairband around his wrist. Inexplicably. So she's still there. That's all he cared about. So why should he worry?

Day 1,883. Let's call it that. A happy medium. The number floats in my head. Krakatoa erupted in 1883. And Karl Marx died in London. Died at his desk of bronchitis and pleurisy. What even is pleurisy? Something about the chest. An olden-day disease. Like scurvy. Like polio and the plague. Our modern-day diseases are much less exotic. More neurotic.

They're in our heads. They're unseen, stealthy buggers that corrupt us in new, insidious ways. They creep in our ears while we're sleeping and bring the contagion with them. Stress, anxiety, depression. Horrid little words. Shameful words. That's their trick. They make us ashamed of ourselves. Lifestyle diseases, we call them. Even that softens them, discredits and dismisses them. But underestimate them at your peril. They can be equally as lethal as what went before. Not them. But what they make us do.

So there I am driving away. Look again and I'm climbing up these stairs, passing Flo, I didn't know her as Flo then. I'm opening the door to this flat. I'm pleasantly surprised. I'm walking across the floor to the window and gazing out. I'm looking at the beach and the sea beyond and the tankers that are no more than grey blobs breaking the horizon. I turn around and see the chair, the kitchen, the short hallway. I'm thinking this will do very nicely, thank you. As bolt-holes go. I put my bag down. Yes, for a short interlude, a place to stop for a month or two until the next stage starts, this will do very nicely. I even start whistling. The hairband is still around my wrist. I take it off and flick it across the room. I rush after it and am not becalmed until I've found it again.

Look again. It's Day 1,883. I'm still here.

'What should I do now?' But Flo doesn't answer. Flo has gone.

I went to the beach. I wanted to find Old Silverback. I had an urge. Not like that. And there he was. Good as gold. It's like he was there waiting for me. As soon as I descended the stairs leading to the sand I saw him again. He was beneath the promenade. Half in shadow and half not. I wondered if that was some sort of metaphor for his life. I think these pointless things now. I search for symbolism. For hidden meanings and missed clues. I make connections between unrelated things. It's just where he stood. It's just where the sun was in the sky.

He stepped forward when he saw me and smiled. I smiled also. I began to walk towards him. Or stride. I didn't wait for his *come hither*. His smile quickly faded and he began to back away. I raised my hand, showing him my palm. I meant it to mean stop but he must have thought it was goodbye, because he turned from me and began walking in the opposite direction. I followed him. He looked over his shoulder and quickened his step. I quickened mine.

'Hey,' I shouted.

He was only about twenty yards in front of me. When he saw me running he started to run also. I passed where he'd been standing and could smell his cologne still in the sea air. I thought I'd catch him easily but Old Silverback had a turn of pace about him. The gap between us widened instead of shortened. I was panting.

'Hey!' I shouted again.

I realised I'd not catch him. I stopped. I wasn't going to hurt him. He must have feared that. Perhaps he thought that I'd let shame take over me. In the quiet hours. When I was mulling over our first encounter. Stilted as it was. Maybe he thought I wanted to take it out on him. He couldn't have been more wrong. I had been thinking about that day. Since I no longer had Flo as my refuge. He was right about that. But the conclusion I'd drawn was not what he feared. Actually, I thought I had probably missed a trick. That I should have let him save me. In his own wicked way. I won't get carried away now and project more than there was. But I see him now with his long limbs, long hair and loin-cloth. There was something of the Jesuses about him. Maybe I needed converting. I should have stayed to find out. That's the nub of it. I was intent on staying the second time. And if he wanted to get on his knees, or wanted me to get on mine, well, any port in a storm. I'm that teenage girl again, trading things she doesn't want for things she does.

'Wait!' I shouted after him. 'Please!' But he didn't stop running. I watched him disappear down the beach.

I saw a dead seagull on the way back. Signs in the sand, see? I saw the flies around it first, then I saw what they had been attracted to. There was only half of him left. The other half had been carried away by the creepy crawlies that were still busy beneath his skeleton. When I crossed the road I looked up at the chimney. The chicks were there. Still grey and still calling hungrily. The rooftops around them were empty.

'That wasn't him,' I shouted up at them reassuringly. But I didn't know that.

And now I'm just sitting in this chair. It's the only chair in the room. I'm not quite sitting. Not anymore. I've slid down it by degrees. Now my arse is hanging off the front and my neck is bent double, folding my chin into my chest. My legs are splayed out in front of me and my arms are hanging over the armrest like two dead things. They're not even mine. When did I go to the beach? Not yesterday. The day before yesterday? Or the day before that? What does it matter? I've been here for days. I know that much. I've hardly moved. I got up to feed a few times. And to piss and shit. But I'm not even bothering with that anymore. I've pissed myself three, maybe four times. The shame of it. But I feel no shame. I'm enjoying it. The decadence. The sense of abandoning all pretence at decorum. First there was just a drop. It came out before I could stop it. I looked down and saw the dark circle arrive on my trousers. I was holding the rest in, but I thought to myself, *why should I?* So I just relaxed and let my bladder empty. I watched the wet stain spread out and I didn't react at all. Warm. Of course it was warm. It had been inside me. Warm on my thighs and on my stomach and under my belt. Warm, but then very quickly turning cold. No matter. A few hours later I did it again and the warmth was back. The cushion under me is soaked now. It is soaked under my arse and in the small of my back, even though I haven't pissed there. One day I'll look back on this moment and be disgusted in myself. Not now. Now I've not got the energy. I begrudge even the effort of breathing. But I'm not breathing. Breathing is a verb. A doing word. And I'm not doing anything. I'm just sat here with my mouth slightly open letting the air do the work. I'm just a receptacle, letting it drift in and out of me like it does any open space.

Get outside. Get the sun on you. Get some exercise.

All my energy has leaked out with the piss. My eyelids are hanging half down over my eyeballs. My entire world is squeezed into a narrow slit on the other side of the room. There are the pizza boxes. Dozens of them in two neat stacks against the far wall rising almost to the ceiling. Each one represents a day. *Fucking pig. You complete fucking pig.* The empty dog basket. *Don't worry. He'll come back when he's hungry. Maybe he ate the pizzas. Filthy beast.* I let my eyes roll to the right, towards the window. It's raining on the other side. I can see it and hear it. Beyond the window the lights of the tankers glimmer dimly in the dullness. My eyelids shut a little further. Almost all the way.

I'm pissing again. For fuck's sake. I've not drunk enough for all this to come out of me. Maybe I have a terminal illness. We can be discovered together. Flo and I. A tragi-comedy. How very Greek. Derek said he was coming back. So where is he? The Great White Hope. He needs to come and put an end to this. I can smell Flo through the walls. Maybe it's me. It's Day 1,884. I know that. I lied about not knowing.

Now my eyelids do shut all the way.

Chapter Twenty-Six
Now

'Happy birthday. I can't believe you're a teenager already.' I'm on the phone to her. This is last year.

'I am now. It's official.'

'How are you?'

'Fine thank you. Are you okay?'

'Yes, thank you.'

Children at nine are remade by thirteen. I have no idea who Grace is anymore. I imagine her in her room, listening to music, writing angsty poems about being in love or not being in love. But that's not her. That's every thirteen-year-old. That's who she is now. I'm so out of touch. Chicken burgers were her favourite food. Are they still? Yellow was her favourite colour. Although she refused to wear yellow. Is it still? Her favourite song was 'White Christmas' by Bing Crosby. She called him Bill.

'It's been so long since I saw you.' This is me talking again.

'Yes, it has.'

'You must send me a picture or I'll forget what you look like. Hahaha.' Silence. We used to talk so freely. If anyone told me that we – her and I, Grace and I, my daughter and I – would become these people I'd have laughed them out the house. She'd have laughed with me. I can see us doing it. Her laughter would have made me laugh harder, and she'd have laughed at my laughter and we'd have kept laughing after whoever had said it had been forgotten. I look around my flat. I imagine her here. I couldn't bear it.

I hear a man's muffled voice on the phone. She says she knows, but not to me. To me she says: 'I have to go now, Daddy.'

'Okay, my friend.'

Another painful silence. We still love each other. I have to believe that. I believe that is what she is waiting to hear during this silence. That's also what I'm waiting for. The silence lingers. We are both hurt. We blame each other. The phone goes click. It gets harder to say each time.

Chapter Twenty-Seven
Now

I am standing by my door. My ear is pressed to it. I am waiting for it to start banging. When it does, I won't fall away. Like I did last time. Lying silently on the floor, hardly breathing, until I'm eventually left alone again. That feeble response. No. Not this time. I've made a decision. I'm ready now. It will end today. He will end it. He doesn't know that yet. He doesn't even know there is something that needs ending. That's his problem. He has no idea what's expected of him.

Him. His problem. How do I even know it's him out there? Derek. The Great White Hope? It could be anyone. It couldn't. It's Derek. It can only be Derek. I whisper his name into the wood. I repeat it until it doesn't make any sense. I listen to how stupid it sounds, with those two dense, clunky syllables. Deh-rek. What a shower of a name. Flo, you did your boy a disservice there, with that. I knew a Derek at school. He had pimples that he used to pick the heads off. He'd get what was inside them, pus, blood, on his fingertips and then chase people around the playground. He never chased me. I wanted him to. I wished for it. Just to see what would happen. I've always felt like there is a certain reaction inside me. It's still there. Coiled. Waiting only for the right provocation.

The silly thing is I was actually quite happy earlier. Quite relaxed. I was sat on the chair in a sort of wake-sleep. My eyes were open. I was staring without consciousness. Parts of my body were twitching with thoughts that were so deep inside me I wasn't even aware I was thinking them. There but not there. I couldn't say how long I'd been like that. Minutes. Hours. Time is distorted. He didn't need to disturb the peace like this. *Bang, bang, bang*, he went. *Bang, bang, bang*. It jolted me. From being comfortably sedated I was suddenly sat forward on the edge of my chair, staring around me in dishevelled confusion. The pizza boxes were no longer in neat piles to the ceiling but scattered across the floor – how? – the dog basket was not where I'd left it, but upside down with its cushions gone – where? *Bang, bang, bang*. I decided to ignore him. I sat back in my chair. I tried to regain the same position but couldn't get comfortable. The surfaces were suddenly cold. My wet trousers were suddenly cold. Every time I tried to settle down I became aware of a new itch. *Bang, bang, bang. Bang, bang, bang*. I reached behind me and pulled out two pillows and shoved them against my ears. They were wet with piss. They smelled of it. I threw them across the room and put my fingers in my ears. That never works. It never stops the sound. So why do we do it? *Bang, bang, bang*. Break her fucking door down, if it means so much to you. I tried to focus on my breathing. In through the nose. Out through the mouth. Clean white air coming in, dirty brown air going out. I know my meditation. In, out, in, out. *Bang, bang, bang*. I shook my head. I stood up. That's when I decided. Enough is enough. It ends today.

The floorboard creaks. He's just out there. I can hear him muttering and mumbling to himself. He's not banging on her door anymore. Perhaps he's staring at mine. Considering it. Well, I'm right here. I'm right fucking here.

'I'm looking for my mother,' he says. 'Doris.'

The first thing I think is how short he is. Much shorter than I imagined. After everything she's told me about him. I expected someone magnificent, imposing. He is imposing. But not like that.

'Well I'm not her,' I say.

'No. She lives there.' He turns to stare at Flo's door. Gestures inanely at it. 'But I don't think she's home.'

'So why are you still here then?'

I'm surprised by how much I hate him. Immediately. With a deep, instinctive revulsion. It's so visceral I can hardly stand here talking to him. He isn't even paying me the courtesy of looking at me. He's looking past me. Into my flat. Poking at my things with those small black eyes. Rodent eyes. Leaving germs on everything they see. I lean into his vision and raise my eyebrows at him. He smiles bashfully. He asks if I am The Gentleman Next Door. The one Doris told him about.

'Don't call your mother Doris. It's disrespectful.'

He ignores this. Which makes me think I didn't say it. He says he's glad to meet me. That's a lie. He holds out his hand. Says it's nice to know someone is looking out for her.

'I'd love to have her with us, she's eighty-nine, but she won't hear of it. She is still so independent.'

She was independent, Derek. Was. I don't say this. I will let him find out for himself. He still has that dumb smile on his face. I can't abide it any longer.

'Look at this,' I say. I point into my lap. I watch with satisfaction as his face changes as he registers the urine stain.

Surprise first, then disgust. 'Yep. I've been pissing myself for days.'

Now I'm the one smiling. It's turning into a good day. The day it will all come to an end. I wonder how it will end. I've not decided. The possibilities are endless. I may even end it in prison. For what though? What have I done that they can know for sure? Failure to report a crime? What crime? Derek has taken a step backwards. He takes another one. He's hovering on the top stair. Around his feet are the broken pot plants. The rich soil has spilled out into little heaps. Some of the flowers are still trying to grow out of them. Others have fallen loose and lie dead on the carpet. I take a step after him.

'Erm, excuse me? Where are you popping off to?'

'I think I'd better come back another time.'

'You don't want to see your dear old mum?' I take another step forward. I'm close enough now so he's standing in a cloud of my piss. 'You're here now. Seems silly to have come all this way.'

'Oh no, it's no trouble at all.'

No trouble at all, he says. No trouble. That riles me. If it's no trouble then why... never mind.

'She's not even home,' he adds.

'Oh yes. She's inside.'

He hesitates. He is confused. I wonder which of those simple words he doesn't understand. 'What?'

'Your mother. She's in there.'

'But I've been knocking.'

'I know you have. Don't rush off. She looks forward to your visits so much. She'd hate for you to go without seeing her.' I put a hand on his arm. 'We both would.' I smile at him. It's a genuine smile, even though my hatred has intensified in the last few minutes. I lead him away from the stairs. He is compliant. 'I have a key. She gave me one. Come on. I'll get it for you.'

I don't release his arm. We walk into my kitchen. I open the drawer nearest the fridge. A few batteries roll to the front. There is a ball of string. Isn't there always? There is a lid for a pen. But no pen. Sheets of paper. Instruction manuals and flyers. In amongst them is a key. I take it out and hold it up.

'Ta-da.'

He takes it from me dubiously. He wants to know why I have a key but doesn't ask.

'She gave it to me ages ago,' I say. 'In case anything happened to her and I needed to get in there.' I turn him around and guide him to the landing. I put my hand on his back and nudge him forwards. 'Go on.'

He is fiddling with the lock now. It's an awkward one. You have to jimmy it a bit. Lift and pull. There is a knack. I don't tell him this. I'm too busy savouring the apprehension. He turns to me doubtfully. I nod again. Perhaps he's struggling because he's shaking so much. There is a sweat patch under his arm. It's not even warm today. I consider helping him. I used to imagine my reaction while it was still happening. While Derek was running around the playground. Derek with the pimples, that is. I'd watch him chasing them about while imagining him coming up behind me and rubbing his grubby finger down my cheek. I could almost feel the air cold on the wet smear. I'd see him smiling at me a fraction of a second before I set upon him. My imagination always skipped to the end then. It missed out the middle bit. It went straight to the part where he is lying on the ground with pulp for a face and the other kids are standing around me in awe. I always thought, rightly or wrongly, that Derek used to imagine the exact same thing. That's why he never came after me.

Ah. He's done it. The lock. I don't need to help him after all. His hand is on the handle. He's turning it. Any moment now. I take a deep breath. As soon as the door opens he buckles. His hands clasp his knees. He coughs. I see him spit. On his own mother's carpet. That's also disrespectful. He looks at me over his shoulder.

'Inside,' I say. I taste the smell when I open my mouth. It's tangible. It's almost like an actual substance. He stands up and walks into the flat. I back away, into my own. I am just waiting. At first there is nothing. There is nothing at all for much longer than I expect. I'm on the verge of going after him when the silence is finally broken. It's just a short burst of sound. Only one syllable. It's like a yelp or a bark. But not exactly either of these things. It's a single ball of shock that bursts out of him. I try to picture what he's looking at. A seething mass of something that is trickling over the chair, down its back and legs, adding to the puddle on the floor.

'Have you found her then?'

Relief. That's what I feel above all else. At last. My secret has been shared. The burden will be lifted. Whatever happens now will happen. The kitchen drawer is still open. Things like that disturb me. I walk into the kitchen to close it. When I come back Derek is in the doorway. Good lord, look at him. I don't know how he is even standing upright. He is so white there can't be a single blood cell above his shoulders. He wants to know what I've done to his mother. It's a reasonable question. I think carefully about my response. I decide to say I've done nothing, nothing at all, that it's just Old Father Time that's done it. I insist that my only action has been inaction. He doesn't believe me. He's crying. He thinks I killed her. I shrug my shoulders.

'You should've come to see her.'

He stops crying. He looks at me. I watch fascinated as the rage sets on his face. He starts to scream as he begins charging at me. In this exact instant I decide to let him kill me. I'm not scared. I'm resigned. Relieved. I've said that. Remorseful. If I could have told Grace I loved her. One last time. One thing I'm not, though, is scared. I think all this in a fraction of a second. Then I close my eyes, put out my hands, and wait for my fate. But nothing happens. He should be upon me by now. I open my eyes. He has stopped. Just over there. He is looking at my hand. I look also. I'm surprised to see it holding a heavy glass ashtray. It's square, with sharp corners. I wonder what it's doing there. I look at Derek. A funny thing happens then. His expression completely changes. The anger drains away and in its place comes doubt, then fear. I am a little mesmerised, if I'm honest, by the effect. I've not said a word. And it's more than fear. It's terror. He knows for certain now, at the same time I do, that this isn't going to end well for him. He backs away but the wall is behind him. He looks to his left and right. He's trapped. I'm walking towards him. He looks paralysed. He's not even going to try and escape. At the last moment he makes a run for it. Unfortunately for him, though, he runs the wrong way. He runs right into the solid mass that is speeding up towards him. It catches him square between the eyes. In the split second of contact I can feel how hard his skull is. But it's not as hard as the glass. There is no give in the glass at all. But there is give in his head, particularly as it jolts backwards.

'She really loved you,' I say. He's on the ground now. I'm standing above him. There is no blood at all. 'She spoke about you all the time. She kept waiting for you. Even I waited a few times. Why didn't you come? Whimpering isn't an answer.'

He rolls onto his belly. He drags himself along the carpet towards the door. I let him get most of the way there then I walk past him and close the door. He starts crying again. He is trying to get up. He is making a good fist of it, too. He's managed to pull his knees up beneath him. But his balance isn't there and he tips sideways. He tries again. He's beside the chair now. He uses it to support his weight. There'll be piss on his hand now. There is still no blood. Not a drop. I almost can't believe I've hit him. But then how did that dent in his forehead get there? He's made it to his feet. He's holding on to the wall as he edges towards the door. But that's where I am.

I pause the scene. I have time. He's not going anywhere. I stop to consider this situation. This is the moment where I decide. I said I was still deciding how this was going to end. Well, this is the moment to do it. What are my options? I still have many. Option One. I call an ambulance. I sit down and wait. Derek will recover. Derek will probably recover. This is the most sensible option. Option Two. Because his injury might be time sensitive, I bundle him in the car and take him to hospital myself. Hand myself in at the same time. Accept my comeuppance. Also sensible. Actually, I'm quite proud of myself. How I can remain so calm. It's easy, if you detach yourself from your surroundings and consider the situation dispassionately. See, Dolores? I can do it, too. Option Three. Get in the car and drive away and never come back. I dismiss this almost immediately. Option Four. Phone Grace. Confess all. Do what she tells me to do. I dismiss this too. Unfair on her. And she'd only pick one of the first two options anyway. So that only leaves one more option. Option Five. The right option.

I look at him in front of me. Pressed against the wall. He's not trying to get to the door now. He knows I'm here. In his way. Still no blood. I listen to the noise he's making. It's wet. Maybe the blood is in his throat.

'Your mother loved those pot plants,' I say. Another sob.

I am aware of how much I hate Derek. But not just Derek. I hate this flat too. And the piss on the chair and on my clothes. I hate the Silverback. Perhaps I did mean him harm. I hate the beach and those great hulking tankers out there sucking the earth dry. I hate those bleating fucking seagulls on the roof. I hate pizza. But I'll still order more tonight. I hate the girl who answers the phone and laughs behind her hand at me. I hate the last five years and most of the years before them. I hate how cruel children can be to their parents. We try our best. We make mistakes. So what? The pain they dish out though. Without mercy. I hate Dolores. She was always going to leave. I hate my dog. Even he preferred someone else. That's my dog. Mine. He got his comeuppance too. I hate the eight billion. Myself most of all. But I can't stay under the water long enough. So I hate Derek most of all. He is the only one here. Yes. Option Five. It's all going to be unleashed on him. That's what my gut says. And we have to follow our guts now, don't we? The fucking Aborigines said so.

'It's no trouble for me either.' I raise the ashtray high above my head. 'No trouble at all.' Lucky Flo. Her son is finally on his way to her.

Chapter Twenty-Eight
Now

I am not shocked by what I've done. Perhaps rather I am in shock. I still feel nothing. I went into the bathroom, once he finally stopped moving. He did put up a fight in the end. He did try to wriggle away from his fate. I had to go after him. *Bang, bang, bang.* My turn now. I looked in the mirror, expecting to see signs of it on my face. They say it changes you forever. Yet I seemed just the same. I studied my eyes. There was nothing in them that hadn't already been there. I washed the blood off my hands and face and plucked out whatever the solid thing was in my eyelashes. Then I examined myself again. Closer this time. From all angles. I looked away and turned back suddenly. Hoping to catch unawares whatever it was I was concealing. But there was nothing.

I'm squatting beside him now, trying to decide what to do next. There was a killer in the eighties I think who cut his victim up and during the course of a day burnt the parts in his little fireplace. They only got him because he confessed. But I want them to find his body. His corpse. His cadaver. Such words. So evocative of rot and ruin and wretchedness. They have to find him or this will never end. He was meant to end it. The Great

White Hope. He failed me. But he can still be useful posthumously. I'm thinking either the beach or beside a road. Not original, I know. But I want to leave him where he'll be found quickly. I don't want this to go on forever. I know, I know. I could pick up the phone and end it right now. I'm not so brave. I can set in motion the chain of events that will inevitably result in the end. But I can't bring myself to directly initiate the ending. There's no difference, really. The difference is just time. But there you are.

———

I'm in the car now. He is in the boot. I didn't even wait for it to get dark. I lugged him out there in broad daylight. Anyone could've seen me. I had half an idea of driving out to where I used to walk Reggie and finding my ditch with the tree trunk. I'm not so far away. But he might be there for weeks. I can't wait that long. No. I'm going a few miles out of town. I'll pull into the first layby I see and whether there is another car there or not, that's where he'll be deposited.

It's stopped raining now. People have emerged from their lairs. I like this town. It's parochial. I'm lucky to be here really. There are children on bicycles on the pavement right beside me. That one has an ice cream. It's too cold for that. There is a mother pushing a pram. And smoking behind it. Tut tut. She can't even be twenty. I stop at the lights. There is a procession passing by. Some sort of street party. The people are dressed from a bygone era. I look at the military uniform. It's from the forties. That old biddy has a check shirt and a flower in her hair. I wind the window down to listen to the music. Simpler times. They move on. The lights change. This is the posh part of town. The houses here are set well back. They gaze out over wide, lush lawns. Some of the driveways wind themselves behind the houses and reappear on the other side. There is a policeman on a motorbike behind me. He's been there for a mile or more. I'm not changing course for him. I pass a school. A few more blocks of houses. Then the town stops abruptly. I look in the rear-view mirror. The policeman is still there. I don't care. I could drive right over him and his bike. I'm trying to think where the layby is. It's not far from here. At this time of day it will be too early for truckers or young couples with dirty deeds on their minds. Ah. There it is. I indicate. The policeman is still behind me. Maybe the end is closer than I thought.

I pull in and his bike goes straight on. I'm relieved and disappointed in equal measure. There is no one else here. I stop the car and get out. I open the boot and look down. I've not even wrapped him in a blanket. He's leaked on Reggie's basket. *Sorry, Reggie. I'll wash it. Promise.* I lean down and lift him up. I don't mind about the blood getting on my shirt. The blood and other things. It was there already. I carry him to the verge and drop him at my feet. He lands awkwardly, sort of bounces, his head does, and then comes to rest on his back with one arm bent unnaturally beneath him and the other across his chest, as though he's feeling in a shirt pocket for something.

Should I say something? A half-baked eulogy. I recite a few lines in my head and they sound fake, hollow. I turn away and walk to the edge of the road. He's easily visible even from here. He's right there. He can't be missed. I watch as one, two, three cars drive by. Not one of the drivers even looks at me. At my clothes covered in blood. Other things. I walk back to my car and get in. I pull out and onto the road that leads back to the town. From now on, the clock is ticking.

Chapter Twenty-Nine
Now

I get out the car and walk towards the front door. The beach on my left. The fronts of the houses on my right. I pass people. They don't notice me. Are they not looking? Can they not see all this? I want to shake them. All apart from one boy. He can't be more than five. He is hanging off his mother's arm. He pulls her to a stop as he stands there staring. I jut my face at him and he shrinks back. But he can't stop looking. I was like that when I was his age. I've already passed him by the time his mother drags him away. She saw nothing. Head in her phone. That's us nowadays. Staring at screens while life passes by. Or death in this case. I open the door and go in. The smell. Holy Christ. I climb the stairs holding my nose. The last time I climbed them I was someone else. I am completely changed now. I know it but I don't feel it. My eyes start to water. From the smell. At the top of the stairs I see both doors are open. I listen for voices inside. If I wait here someone in a uniform will come bustling out. There is no one up there though. The doors are open because I left them open. My hands were too full of Derek. I close her door. I try not to think of all the times I went through it.

Something smells good.

Only I've made far too much of it again.

Good times. I look at the pot plants. The soil is dry. The leaves are wilting. I'm confused. I'm sure it's not been so long.

I enter my own flat and walk directly into the kitchen. I'm standing at the sink. I notice the drawer is still open too. But I closed it? There is the battery and the ball of string and the lid with no pen. I hit it with my hip. The drawer shudders and everything inside jumps up out of fright. I walk back onto the landing with the jug and begin watering the poor plants. *I saw you. I'll save you.* Ever the superhero. I keep pouring until the jug is completely empty. I go back inside, refill it, and do it again. I don't know how many times I do this. I stop counting. When I'm finished, the piles of sand are muddy puddles. Streams trickle over the carpet away from them... like they used to for her.

Finally satisfied, I go back inside and shut the door behind me. I survey the room. I take in the mess he's left on the carpet and wall. Half the floor space seems contaminated with him. He really did resist then. I don't remember it. I remember the first blow. How it felt when one hard object hit another slightly less hard object. He was just over there. Propped up by the wall. That explains the stain. I don't know about the rest of it though. I'm racking my brains. I see an image of him on his hands and knees. My hand is in the image too, grabbing a fistful of hair. I don't know if it's real or if I've just imagined it. There is something on the floor. Up against the skirting board. It appears to have rolled there. I suspect it's the main mass from which the thing I found in my eyelashes came. My hand reaches up, strokes the eye absently.

I step back. Away from all this. I sigh. I suddenly feel very heavy in myself. I can't begin cleaning all this now. It will have to keep for another day. I just want to sit down. I turn my back on the chair and bend my knees. I remember the piss in the nick of time and arch away.

Part of me wonders why I care. I'm covered in blood and brain. I can't figure myself out sometimes. Instead, I cross the floor and fold myself into Reggie's bed. I have to pull my knees up under my chin to fit all the way in. I hold my legs in place. I start to rock. It's like I'm on a small boat at sea. When I was very young I used to pretend the carpet was an ocean, full of sharks. I'd jump from one chair to the next. I think I'd like to play that game again now. I hear myself chuckling.

They'll call me a psychopath. They'll blame me for next door too. Just like Derek did.

I have an idea. I reach for a pizza box, one of the many here, and stand it on its side next to me. I balance another one next to it. And another. It doesn't take long before I've constructed walls on three sides. I reach over them for more boxes to use as the roof. I open the boxes up and lay them across the top, then lay myself down inside the tunnel. I could have said coffin. Inside the tunnel. Only my head is sticking out. It's on the side where the window is. I can see stars out there. Thousands of them. I stare at them until it dawns on me that the sky is clear. The clouds have gone. The calm after the storm. Is that right? I don't think that's right. I'm only half here. Most of me is waiting for it to sink in.

All those stars though. We tell ourselves that our dearly departed have become stars. That's a lot of dead people. *Hello, Flo. Hello, Derek.* And do you really see stars if you're struck on the head, or is that just for the comic books? I'm staring at them all though, and I'm beginning to calm down. My breathing is slowing. My hands are still shaking. But not like they were. I've tucked them under my body. It's because I am realising that what I've done today won't matter. Not in the grand scheme. It's a simple matter of scale. The stars have made me see it all so clearly. There are eight billion people on the earth and I'm only one of them. But it's even better than that. The earth is only one of eight planets in the solar system. And our solar system is only one of 100 billion in the galaxy, and our galaxy is only one of 200 billion in the universe. Give or take. Do you see the shrinkage? Greater with each new extrapolation. My moment is reduced in meaning to nothingness. I've even heard, and I don't know if it's true, that our universe is only one of dozens in a multiverse. So everything is repeated again and again and again. And here I am, fretting about a single act on a single day committed by a single person. That breeze that blew our bedroom curtains when we were kids, we're that. We're not even that.

I might sleep in this den. It's comfortable enough. It's so much better than the ones I made as a boy. When the ocean had transformed into a desert. They were just blankets draped over chairs pinned to the top of tables by big books. Rudimentary stuff. I loved being inside them though. There's my mother's face. Upside down in a triangle of light. She's telling me it's time for dinner. I'm not ready yet. I pull the flap down again and hold it down. I'm not ready yet. I don't want to come out. I close my eyes. I'm not a bad man.

I can hear the wind. I think it was the wind that woke me. It's pitch black. Outside and in here. I'm worrying about the seagull chicks up on the roof. They could get blown off in this weather. I don't know if they can fly yet. I saw one on the road the other day. He didn't fly away when I approached. I think now it's because he couldn't. I'm stupid. I didn't check on them when I got home yesterday. I checked on the plants but forgot about them completely. And now it's bothering me. That dead bird on the beach wasn't their father. I'm certain of it. I want to get up and go outside. It's suddenly very important to me that a parent is there with them. I don't suppose I'd even be able to see them in the dark. I lie still. I wait it out and the urgency passes.

There is light in the room now. Warm yellow light. Not the dull grey of dawn. My face is tipped to it and being warmed by it. I am still in the den. It's still standing. Incredibly I can't have moved an inch during the night.

'If you lash out the walls will come tumbling down.' I say this out loud. My voice in the silence startles me.

Maybe I am a psychopath. I don't even know what the word means. Medically speaking. Prone to random acts of social violence. I'd say that what I did was more antisocial. But I understand the point. Lack of empathy and remorse. Well, I do lack empathy. But we all do. Ours is not an empathetic species. Cruelty is part of us. We're cruel when we're alone and we're cruel in a crowd. Learn history. Listen to the news. A man threw his baby in the river yesterday. If a lack of empathy describes a psychopath, then I think that's just about all of us. And remorse? A lack thereof? I don't know about that yet. It's too soon to tell.

What I do know is that if I am a psychopath then I didn't start out that way. I never took magnifying glasses to insects or stuffed fireworks up the arses of cats. I'd never have countenanced such barbarity. So, there must be a tipping point. A moment I can identify and say, there, that's it, if that hadn't happened, or if it had happened differently, then none of this would have happened either.

Yesterday was the tipping point. There doesn't need to be a slow build-up. What I did was enough all by itself. It will be the start, middle and end of me. It will obliterate everything else. I will be that act and I will be nothing else ever again.

I sit up suddenly. The den collapses around me. I could get in the car right now and drive away. Option Three. How far would I get? I might get as far as Grace. I could be there when she finishes school. She'd see me and come running and the last five years would fall away just like that. *Come on, little friend. We're off. I'm sorry. Let's let bygones be bygones. Life's too short.* Or words to that effect.

I lie back down. A box breaks under me. A hard corner jabs my back. I roll onto my side, away from the mess that is still on the carpet and the walls, and start retching. Nothing comes out. The shock is wearing off. My whole body is trembling now. I tell myself they're wrong, that I'm not a psychopath, that yesterday hasn't turned me into one. No single grain of sand defines the sand dune. Then I tell myself that even if they're right it doesn't matter anyway. I try to remember my argument about the stars and space. I can't do it. It doesn't add up anymore. It makes no sense at all. I will be my actions. No. Not my actions. I will be just that one action.

Chapter Thirty
Now

Dear Daddy,

Yes, I am writing to you again. After all this time. Are you surprised to hear from me? Did you even notice when I stopped writing so often and then stopped completely? If you did you didn't say, so I guess you didn't care.

This is a good start, isn't it! Can you tell how angry I am? Maybe I shouldn't write to you in this mood, but I get in this mood whenever I think about writing to you, and I've been putting it off for so long I just want to get it over with and then it's all out of my head. This is actually the fourth time I've tried to write this letter. I didn't finish the first one. I started shouting at you and then I just the ripped the paper apart. I screwed up the second and third letters too. Before I finished them. So let's see how this one goes.

Pierre is here this time. Sitting on the bed. That might help because he calms me down. He is my boyfriend. You didn't even know that, did you? We've been going out for eight months. Mum likes him too, because he's so polite. He's only got a dad so between us we've got a full set. We joke about it, but neither of us laugh. It helps though, that he sort of understands what it's like. I sometimes don't even have to say and he just knows what I'm thinking.

You should thank him. It's his idea that I'm writing to you. He says I'm only responsible for what I do and that I'll regret it if I don't do everything I can. Even if I don't think I will now. He's very wise for sixteen. Mum doesn't mind either way. Whether I write. She says she doesn't want to interfere in my relationship with you. Relationship, Mum? She shrugged her shoulders at that. She says as long as I don't get upset if you don't write back, then it's up to me. I will get upset. So what? I'm writing anyway.

Well, I've only written a page and I've not even properly started. That's because I don't know how to start. I know sort of what I want to say, but I don't know how to start saying it. Pierre says it doesn't matter. To just write what comes into my head and you'll understand.

Okay, so what's in my head right now at this very moment is that you're the worst dad ever. You're even worse than dads that have died. At least they have an excuse. I've actually started telling people that you died. Then they don't talk about you anymore. What do you think about that? I keep imagining seeing you again. You know what I'd do, I would just start punching you. And screaming at you. I wouldn't feel bad about it either. You deserve it. I bet that's what you're so scared of. I've just sworn out loud. Pierre wants to know why. I told him it doesn't matter why.

Do you even know why I'm angry? Do you even care? You probably think it's because you and Mum split up and kids get angry about that all the time and it's just a normal reaction. Actually, I don't care that you got divorced. I'm not a baby. Everyone's parents are divorced. So what? But at least they still see their children now and then. At least they do more than send birthday and Christmas cards saying, 'love Daddy'. That means nothing. Everyone knows that means 'from' not 'love'. So what makes you so special? That you can't be bothered to reply to my letters, that you can't be bothered to say more than two words when I phone you. When I used to phone you. I don't bother now, do I? Another thing you've obviously not noticed. Because it's not like you've started phoning me.

I've just sworn again. At you this time. Pierre didn't say anything.

See! This always happens!! I don't even want to write this letter. Why should I? I was going to tell you loads of stuff about what's been going on. I was going to show you how friendly and mature I am now. Well, I'm not going to. I don't want to. What's the point?? You don't care. I don't even care. So there is no point. And you don't even deserve to know!

Pierre is telling me to keep writing. I've just sworn at him too now. And I'm not going to keep writing.

Hello again,

It's the next day. I'm calmer now. I actually feel better for writing all that yesterday. Whether you read it or not. I've just read it over. I want to change a lot of things but Pierre says to leave it exactly as it is, because that's how I truly feel. So I won't start over. But I will start differently. I said about telling you what's happening in my life. I'm going to do that.

But now I'm thinking about what to say, even that's hard. It's been so long since I wrote that I'm not even sure what I've told you. I don't even know what's news and what isn't. I could get upset if I thought about that too long. Moving swiftly on!

So you know about Pierre now. Do you know that I've decided to be a vet? I want to own my own surgery. We'll care for all types of animals, but I personally want to look after horses. I even know what subjects I need to take. I've also become a vegetarian. I can hardly not be. If I'm becoming a vet.

Do you know that I had to move schools because I was being bullied? We had to move houses too because they knew where I lived. Luckily Mum works from home so we could do that pretty easily. I don't see Pierre as much as I used to. Just at weekends. But it's okay. Mum lets him stay over on Saturdays. Just not in my room.

It was really only two girls but they were the most popular girls so it was sort of everyone in the end. Mum thinks it's because I'm English but there were two other English girls in the class and no one picked on them. I'm learning judo now. Because of it. Because I got into a massive fight before we left. They kept hitting me but I didn't feel a thing. I had to see a doctor afterwards. Not that type of doctor. One who deals with 'anger issues'. You know what she told me? She said a lot of children come from broken homes but they don't use it as an excuse for bad behaviour. Can you believe she said that? Then she gave me tablets to help me calm down and sleep better. I don't take them. Like I would after that! Like I'd do anything she suggested.

I'm getting angry again just thinking about it. So what? I don't want to be calm all the time. Why should I have to be? It's boring. No one can make me. If I want to shout and scream sometimes then why can't I? Why should I have to be the good girl all the time, just to make life easier for everyone?? No one is trying to make my life easier, are they? Actually, it's perfect I'm writing to you right now. You're the perfect person to speak to about this. About doing what you want and not caring what anyone else thinks. Because that's what you do, isn't it? You always did. Even before. Is it fun? Does it make you happy? Are you happy living there all by yourself? Do you ever even think of me, or miss me? I used to think it was amazing. How you didn't follow the rules. How you just did things because you felt like it. Mum seemed so boring compared to you. But now I think it's just selfish. And mean. And everyone else has to suffer because of it. Everything is your fault. If I shout and scream. If I need tablets. If I tell people you're dead. It's all your fault...

I'm back. I had to stop for a while. If Pierre wasn't here I'd have torn this up by now. I'm determined I'm going to finish though. But I'll be quick, because it's scary and I don't want to lose it again.

I told you we had to move. It's better at my new school. I'm much happier. My best friend here is from China. Her name is Feng Mian. It means to fall asleep in the woods while listening to the breeze. I like that. They take great care naming their children in China. She's teaching me Chinese. Ni hao ma. It means how are you? If you just say Ni hao it's like hello.

Mum and I are best friends too. Most of the time. Don't tell Feng Mian! But you can have two best friends. I never realised how funny she is. Mum, I mean. Has she always been like that? I don't remember you laughing like I do. She has me in stitches sometimes. Like you used to. Either she's become very funny or I've just started noticing. She's not as silly as you were. She says things with no expression and sometimes you don't even know she was making a joke until afterwards. She does it a lot when we're out. I think it's clever how she makes these sly comments that no one else even notices. But I do. We laugh about them in the car on the way home.

I know that fourteen-year-old girls are meant to hate their mums, but I really like mine. I love her too. But you don't get a choice about that. You sort of have to love your mum, don't you? But you don't have to like her as well, so, I'm very lucky. It's just the two of us most of the time. We tell each other we don't need men. Not when Pierre is here obviously. I sometimes think she's turning me into a feminist. Or I'm turning her into one. Or you have turned us both into one.

I'll give you an example. When Pierre told me I should write to you he explained it by saying that it's better to regret what you've done than what you've not done. I thought that was so true. I told you he was wise. But when I told Mum she said that it's a famous quote. Pierre didn't tell me that. He let me believe he'd said it. It's only a small thing, and maybe he didn't even know someone else had said it first, but I don't trust boys easily so any little thing like that makes me suspicious.

Do I sound older to you? Because I feel it. When I'm not going off the rails. It's like there's been a growth spurt in my head. We're learning about relationships in school. Maybe that's why I feel like I'm older. Mum says I've been through a lot for someone my age and that I should expect my experiences to change me. She says she's proud of how I'm coping – even with the meltdowns and drama.

So, I'm just going to come out and ask it: do you still love me? Because I don't think you do. That's the only thing I can think of to explain why you don't want to see me, or even talk to me. Mum says that maybe you were embarrassed about how you acted. And by the time you weren't embarrassed anymore too much time had passed. She says being close to someone is a habit and you can get out of that habit quickly and then not remember how to get into it again.

I'll tell you a secret that I've not told anyone else, not even Mum: I used to count the days after you left. I got all the way to 1,000. I used to write them down in a book before I went to bed. I had to stop because it was making me so upset I couldn't get to sleep. Even after I stopped counting I couldn't sleep properly. I had to see the doctor about that too.

And if you didn't want to come here then I could always come to you. I've heard Mum tell you that she didn't mind. Do you remember the last time I asked? It was just before I turned thirteen. I wanted to spend my birthday with you. Because I was becoming a teenager. I know you remember. You said you'd arrange something. But you didn't arrange anything. You didn't even mention it again.

So, what am I supposed to think, Daddy? If you do still love me you have a funny way of showing it. Everyone keeps telling me that what happened had nothing to do with me. I used to believe that. I really did. I used to think you had just left Mum. But now I think you left us both. And that's the real reason I get so angry. Because I don't know what I did that was so wrong.

And then I get angry at Mum when she tries to defend you. Not like Charmaine's mum. Charmaine is another one of my friends. Only she's not my friend anymore. She is one of the girls who bullied me. Her parents are also divorced. That's why we became friends. She hates her dad, but only because of what her mum's told her about him. I can't remember Mum ever saying a single bad thing about you.

'I don't want to prejudice your relationship with your father. That's not fair on either of you. He's your father. Your relationship with him is your own business.'

That's what she said just after you left. I remembered it word for word, even though I didn't know what prejudice meant. I sort of do now, but not properly. Maybe I'm not as grown up as I thought I was and when I'm older I'll understand it better. For now, all I know is that I'm fourteen and you've not seen me since I was nine.

But this letter will decide it for me. If you don't write back this time, and properly, with a proper letter, then I'll know I'm right. But I hope I'm wrong. Because I miss you, Daddy. I remember all the fun times we had together. If I knew that was the last time that I was going to see you I'd have turned around. Do you remember? In my room? I stood at the window watching you drive off. I was sure you'd come back. I waited for so long. I've changed so much since then. I've lived in four different houses. I live in a different country now. I'm a little taller and a lot fatter. But I'm still the same underneath. I'm still waiting at the window.

So please write me back. I don't want to be like Charmaine.

Love Grace

Chapter Thirty-One
Then

Day 34. All the way back to Day 34. I didn't know it as Day 34 yet. I'd not started counting. I'm at the airport. I'm not going anywhere. They are. I'm only here to bear witness. I've been waiting hours when I finally see them. Grace in the middle. Wearing yellow. She never wears yellow. I almost don't recognise her because of it. It's her walk that gives her away. She walks just like me. So I've been told. I don't know how I walk. But I know how she walks. She's drinking Lucozade. At her age. It wouldn't have happened on my watch. I pull down the cap I've bought for this very occasion – men my age shouldn't own caps or football shirts – and watch from under the brim as they pass right by me. I could leave now. Now I've seen them. I consider it. While I was waiting for them to arrive I speculated on what I might do when they did. Doing nothing seemed to be the most likely. Just slipping away quietly. Unseen.

I step out into the crowd and follow them. At one point Grace stops suddenly and turns around. She is looking for me. I know she is. Maybe she senses my presence. She looks right at me. We're no more than twenty yards apart. I freeze. I try to think what to say. Her gaze moves on. Still searching. I realise she didn't see me. How? How did she not? It's the cap. I never wear a cap. I'm not what she's looking for. Dolores and Joe have stopped too. They're waiting for her. Dolores comes back and takes her hand and the three of them continue on together. One big happy family. I'm glad of the crowds now. I can stay close yet keep enough bodies between us. There is a long line waiting to go through security. They join the back of it. I slow as I approach. I'm calculating. I estimate I've got ten minutes until they reach the front. I walk straight past for twenty steps and then double back. As I approach from the other side I look at where I left them but they're not there. I wonder if they were ever there. I look along the line. They're halfway down it already. I'm shocked by how far they've moved. I feel panic rising up inside me. I rub my hands on my trousers. I realise I'm running out of time. I become aware that I'm now just standing here in the middle of the floor staring at them. I must be conspicuous. I back away and find a post to lean against. To hide behind. Joe bends down and says something and Grace laughs. It's not a real laugh. She's only being polite. If he was her real father he'd know the difference. She looks away and the laugh drains instantly from her face. There are only about four groups in front of them now. I'm running out of time. I said I was here to bear witness. It's true. Because I don't fully believe any of this is real. Even now. There is a part of me that won't accept I quit my job, ransacked the house, lost the dog. I didn't walk out. I don't live in the flat. I'm not really here. Any moment now I'm going to be back in the boardroom. My seven workmates – they were never mates – will be staring at me. Some amused. Some disdainful. Yes, Jason. No, Jason. Three bags full, Jason. I'm not so bold. I've never moved forward dynamically my whole life.

Three groups. I'm running out of time. I'm walking towards them now. If any of them turned they would see me. Two groups. I'm nearly there. There is an old couple in front of me. Just behind them. They look at me oddly. I smile. Put my hands out apologetically. I can't speak or Grace will hear my voice. The line shuffles forward again. I shuffle forward with it. One group. I'm so close now if I leaned over this person I could touch them. And then what? I keep my hands by my sides. Grace turns around again. How can she not see me here? I'm so close. I'm right here. I'm staring right at you. But that's just it. I'm too close. She's looking beyond me. Over me. Around me.

'Come on, darling.'

It's Dolores.

I'm running out of time. I need to act now. Someone nudges me from behind. I look down at my feet. They aren't moving. What was that song I always got wrong? *Trying? Tired?* I used to pretend I didn't know. It made us laugh. I'm smiling at the memory. Only now I really don't know. I'm nudged again. I step out of the line. When I look up again they've gone. I've run out of time.

I'm standing in the viewing gallery on the second floor. In front of a huge window that overlooks the mishmash of runways. I can see their plane. Joe is standing right next to me. I can see him in the glass. He is staring at me. I look at the empty Lucozade bottle in his hand. He's meant to be on the plane.

'You're meant to be on the plane,' I say.

He tells me they're just friends, they've only ever just been friends, the rest of it is all in my head. I find myself working hard to disbelieve him. He's so earnest. And so tall. Why does he have to be so tall? He can't help but look down on me. I don't know whether to hug him or punch him. I might punch him if I knew he'd not punch me back.

They'll be sitting down now, buckling up. *Your exits are here, here, and here.* 150–180mph. That's how fast a plane needs to go on take-off. I know this because I'm The Pilot.

'You really don't know what you've lost,' Joe says.

I push him but he doesn't move. He doesn't even sway backwards. My hands bounce off him. He just stands there like some dumb monument. Some monolith to what used to be. I have to say something. I start speaking before I've decided what.

'You don't know anything.' I don't know what that is meant to suggest. He is just looking at me. I imagine he is about to smile. He's smiling on the inside. I must not under any circumstances let him smile at me. 'You don't give nine-year-olds Lucozade. Jesus. What fuckhead does that?'

It's not great. It's the best I can do. But it doesn't matter. I'll not see him again. I'll not see Grace or Dolores again either. But that's another thing I don't know yet.

I pull up outside the flat. The sea is on my left and my new front door is about twenty yards ahead on my right. I open it and begin climbing the stairs, towards my chair and all the empty space I so craved. Flo is there. At her plants. When she sees me she puts the watering can down and walks into her flat. I stop at her open door and look in. She is standing at her kitchen counter stirring something that I am convinced doesn't need stirring.

'Something smells good,' I say.

'Only I've made far too much of it again.'

Chapter Thirty-Two
Now

Day 1,990. These are the things I know: where she lives, how long it will take to get there, that I must leave today. Now.

I stand up. My arse is damp. It's from the chair. I'd forgotten about that, all the pissing. With everything else going on. I'd not forgotten. I assumed it must have dried so I put it out of my mind. It hadn't dried. I didn't feel it sitting down. The warmth must have masked the moisture. I tap the seat of my trousers. A little more than damp. I should change. I don't have time to change. Even though it would take ten seconds.

I walk into my room and retrieve the shoebox from beneath the bed. I don't expect to return here. At the front door I stop and turn around. His mess is still everywhere. I've not cleaned it up. I realise that I never intended to. But I have one more thing to do before I can go. I don't want to do it, but feel I must. For old time's sake. I open her door before I spend too long thinking about it. There are our two comfortable old chairs by the window. There is the small table between them. I begin wading through a fog of putridness that is already leaving a film on my skin. I walk right up to her. She is where I left her, but she has moved. Flo is now no more than a wet shapeless stub that has started leaning over to the right. If they don't find her in time her whole edifice will topple over and land with a splat.

'I'm going to see her, Flo. I won't be coming back. I wanted to tell you, before I leave, that I am proud to have been your friend.'

I know other things: that I'm a killer, that they will come for me, that I will be caught.

I'm in the car now. The old one. I gave her the good one. The key is in the ignition and I'm ready to go. I glance in the mirror and see a police car approaching. I watch it getting closer. It is slowing down. The nearer it gets to me. I hope I'm not too late. I wonder if I should run. I try to picture the moment I'm apprehended. Face-down on the pavement. Hands behind my head then twisted down my back and shoved into handcuffs. It won't be like that. This isn't Los Angeles and I'm not black. I expect it to be an anticlimax. A polite, decorous anticlimax. They will invite me to come with them. I will agree amicably. I make a mental note to count how many times they say please and thank you. The police car wasn't slowing down. It was just the angle that made it seem that way. It passes right by me and I watch it drive away, oblivious to what it's left behind.

I turn the key and the car coughs into laboured life. Only after it's started do I recall the countless times it hasn't. I wait. Every few seconds the engine chokes, clears its throat then settles again. It's not healthy. But it's got one big effort to make yet. I'm waiting to see if the police car is going to circle back. The shoebox is on the seat beside me. It contains all the letters she ever wrote me and the many more I wrote but didn't send her. I had a reason once. For not sending them. I only half remember it. The police car hasn't circled back. It's not going to.

One-nil to me. I check the mirrors then ease out onto the road. I'm heading south.

The cars in front are all too slow. They all see me coming and jump to the side like startled dogs. Don't say dog. A watery sun glistens on the wet motorway and there is a gold ball of light twinkling in the windscreen. I could reach out and take it. It's for you, I'll say, when I get there, a gift. I am trying to imagine only good things. The fairies asked me to give it to you. They say it's magic. Like the bench. They say everyone is good and bad, but this light contains all the good in all the people you've ever met. They want you to have it. She'll take my hand. I must tell you something. It doesn't matter, Daddy. All that matters is that you're here now. Or something like that.

'You left us both. It makes me so angry sometimes.'

Her anger is really hurt. I caused it. I can't dwell on that now, but I wonder how long it will be until that anger comes out. Once she sees me, I mean. It might erupt immediately. I hope not. I hope for a short window to say what I need to. I don't know what that is yet. I don't want to plan ahead and sound contrived. It needs to be spontaneous, heartfelt, instinctive. If she'll let me. But I trust her. We have a rare bond. What was once can be again.

I'm driving much too fast. I can't seem to slow down. I can hear the tyres on the wet surface. I think I can. I pass trees. I don't look right at them. They merge into one long green blur behind the glass. I pass gaps between the trees. Sometimes towns fill the gaps. Sometimes they are just gaps. More trees. More gaps. It will take eleven hours to get there. Ten now. It seems long but after five years it's not so long. Yet I'm impatient. I'm rushing. I'm risking it all at this speed. I don't care. I can't slow down. The further and faster I go the greater the sense of urgency. Urgency can feel a lot like panic. I see that now. I'm not sure if I'm rushing towards something or away from it. They are coming. They are right behind me. They are in my room right now, looking at the mess I left for them. One of them is talking into a radio. Somewhere else there is a computer screen with my name on it. With every passing minute they know more about me. And I hate the time I've wasted. Not the last five years. Although I hate that too. I mean recently. Making that stupid den. Lying in it hour after uncomfortable hour. I lied about sleeping soundly. I stayed glued to the floor, staring wide-eyed at the ceiling while my body went numb. Sitting on that piss-soaked chair while precious more time ticked away. I see myself just sat there like a lump, putting all of this in jeopardy.

I realised I've not even thought about Dolores in all this. Whether she'll be there or not. Whether she'll be welcoming or not. Probably or not. But that's neither here nor there. God help her if she gets in my way.

Everywhere I look now I see police cars. Every flashing light is for me. No. They're just mending the road. It's just another white car. But I know what I know. If not this time, then the next time. I wish I'd dumped him somewhere else. Even just rolling him down the ditch would have bought me a bit more time. I press my foot down harder on the accelerator. It doesn't go down any more. It's already flat on the ground. I become aware of the noise the engine is making. It sounds like a dying horse. I look at the rev counter and the temperature gauge. Neither is working. The needles are stuck. More trees. More gaps. 'Hang in there,' I say. I pat the top of the steering wheel. We're down to nine hours. Eight.

Dolores never loved Grace as much as me. It's unfair that she got her. I used to take her to the park every Sunday morning. She was maybe two or three. I remember there was a ramp up to the top of the climbing frame. It was made of wooden slats all joined together. This one morning, in winter, the wood was slippery with frost. Grace tried to climb up the ramp. There was a rope hanging down to help her, but she wasn't strong enough. Each time she'd get nearly to the top and then slip back on her belly, all the way to the bottom. Time after time. I filmed it. Until she got angry and told me not to. I still have the video somewhere. I never look at it. I keep meaning to. It just sits there in a file taking up memory. I kept telling myself I'd set aside an entire evening and go through all my pictures. I never did. That ramp. Grace climbed it in the end. That morning. I remember that much.

I have to stop now. I have no choice. The petrol light. I noticed it flash on an hour ago and have been trying to ignore it ever since. But I have no choice now. I veer across the lanes and up a slip road. That most definitely is a police car. Parked there at the entrance. I'm not imagining it this time. I try to see inside it as I drive past but its windscreen is full of sky and cloud. I put it out of my mind. I can't change it now. The port, I estimate, is no more than ninety minutes away. Two hours if the traffic is bad. I look at the time. It will be touch and go what ferry I get. But I must stay calm and not rush. No silly mistakes. It doesn't matter which I get. Either way I'll be out of the country by early evening. I'll feel much better then. I stop the car and get out. Petrol, not diesel. I must remember the basics. But where's my wallet? I remember it on the kitchen counter. I feel my pockets. It's not there. I'm staying calm. I look inside the shoebox. I look in the glove compartment. I'm about to start screaming when I see it on its side between the seat and the door. What was it? Petrol. Petrol. Don't be stupid now.

How long is the queue? But it's not the queue at fault, it's the person at the till. I watch him pressing buttons in slow motion. Then he stops completely. He knots his brow. His hand just hovers above the register, uncertain where to go next. The people in front of me are shuffling from one foot to the other. Everyone is suppressing something. He looks up and smiles wanly. Says something pathetic then looks over his shoulder. Someone else appears at his side. They lean over him and press a button – just a single button, simple – and the till pings open. I am willing the second person to go to the other till but they disappear again. I am trying so hard to breathe normally. I realise there is something warm and wet on my fingers and look at them. It's blood. That's how hard I've been scratching my head while this numbskull has been wasting all our lives away.

The police car that had been parked on the slip road pulls into the forecourt and stops behind my car. It might be the same police car. It might not. I didn't notice the licence plate. I see now that there are two people inside.

I shuffle forward with the queue. Numbskull does much better with the next customer and sends her on her way without any alarms. And the customer after her.

I look outside again. No one has got out of the police car. It is still just parked there. I can still see the two figures inside, but I can't see what they're doing.

It's my turn next. But there is another delay. What now? I don't understand how complicated it can be. He's apologising for something now. Who is this person? I swear involuntarily and someone behind me murmurs their agreement. I'll miss the earlier ferry now. Inhale. Hold it. Exhale. The person in front of me leaves.

'Just number two,' I say.

'Anything else, sir?'

'I've just answered that, haven't I?'

'No problem.'

'Why would there be a problem? Why are you talking to me about problems?'

I pay and walk out. The police car has gone. I start to laugh. Two-nil. Someone coming the other way looks at me oddly and I smile and shake my head at them. It's okay, my expression says, and they smile back. I am staring at the empty space behind my car. I almost can't believe it. Another car pulls into it. It's a silver Land Rover. All four doors open at once and a family gets out. I clap once. 'Yes!' I realise I say this aloud. But it's confirmation. I thought for a horrible moment it was over. It doesn't matter about the early ferry. An hour either way won't make any difference. I'm coming, Grace. I'm saying this over and over and over in my head as I get back in the car.

The police car hasn't gone. It's just moved. It's parked on the side of the exit road. Every car here will have to drive straight past it. I just sit here looking at it through the windscreen. One of their heads appears in the gap between the seats. They are looking back at me. The head withdraws again. I put the key into the ignition. It doesn't fit. It scrapes all around it before I can finally force it in. There is something on my cheek. I put my hand to it and look. It's the blood from where I've cut my head. I suck my fingers clean then dry the blood off my face and head with the bottom of my shirt. The police car is still there. I know they know. Okay. Well. I can't sit here all day. I turn the key. Nothing happens. I hear a click, but nothing else. I turn it again. I don't even hear the click this time. This old car. This heap. I gave her the good one. But she flew to France, so where is it? The family is returning to their Land Rover. They are carrying drinks and sandwiches. I watch in the mirror as they all pile back in. I turn the key again. Not a sausage. One of the police officers gets out and starts walking towards me. The Land Rover behind me turns its headlights on. It's ready to go. I can hear its engine. I'm surprisingly calm. I'm actually the calmest I've been in days. Calmness can feel a lot like relief. I turn the key again. I know it won't start now. I think this is nearly over. At last. I'm sorry about Grace. I did really want to get there. I think somehow I knew I wouldn't make it.

I open the car door and start running.

I'm running back the way I came. Away from the police car. I'm on the slip road. I can hear my shoes hitting the ground, my breath bursting out of me like gunshot. On one side are the trees. I'm not going so fast now that I can't see them individually. The sun is setting behind them. Ribbons of gold between the trunks. On the other side is the motorway and all the cars going about their business. I really can hear the sound of tyres on wet roads now. I was only imagining it earlier. I look over my shoulder. The police car is driving after me. A blue light is going round in circles on its roof. Only now am I aware of the siren. I keep running. I can't outrun it. I don't mind. I close my eyes and keep going. I'm overwhelmed by this sense of freedom. I may never run like this again.

Suddenly a huge weight lands on my back and knocks me over. My face hits the ground before I can get my arms up to protect myself and I feel the skin tear off me. But I don't mind about that. Both me and the weight roll over and for an instant I'm on top of him. It's half a chance. But I don't want it. I only want it to be over. I raise my hand as if to strike because that's what's expected of me. I don't strike. I just keep my hand up there, poised, until a second weight hits me from the side and sends me sprawling into the vegetation. My head hits something hard and for a moment I'm dazed. Then they're both on me. They're shouting and each of them has an arm and is yanking it harder than I expected. I wriggle a bit, and their grip tightens until it feels like my bones will be pulled out of their sockets. I realise I was wrong. About the avuncular policemen and their politeness and decorum. About the pleases and thank yous. I don't mind about that either.

Chapter Thirty-Three
Now

'Why did you kill her?'

'I didn't. Why do you keep asking that?'

'Tell us how you killed her then?'

'I didn't kill her.'

He looks up from his notepad and smiles over the rim of his glasses.

'But Mr Smythe, we know you did.'

I'm still here. In this room. I don't know how long it's been. Hours. It feels like days. There aren't any windows letting in the light. And there isn't a clock on the wall. Why isn't there? It's almost like it's deliberate. I thought it would be over quickly. A simple in and out. I thought I'd sit down, tell them what happened and then we'd move on to the next phase of this. Whatever that might be. It's all new. Everything that's happening now is happening for the first time. But it's not been like that at all. They keep asking questions. Questions beget more questions. Most of them I've already answered. Like why did I kill her? 'You mean him,' I said, the first time they asked it. But they really did mean her.

There are four of us here. The one who just spoke has done most of the talking. I can't work him out. I can't decide if he's smart or not. He looks smart. With his spectacles and all the notes he's taking. But then he doesn't seem to be hearing the answers. Or understanding them. And I'm getting confused by all the writing he's doing too. I thought it had to do with what I was saying but I don't know anymore. Because he's writing far more than I'm saying. He keeps writing even when I'm not talking. I'm beginning to suspect that what he's actually writing has nothing to do with this. That he's not even fully engaged. Or listening. That's why he has to keep asking me the same stuff over and over.

Next to him his partner just sits there silently. Observing. Taking it all in. She looks about fifteen. Like she could be a friend of Grace's, the one who hates her father. Chantal. That's what I've been calling her in my head. She's got silver cross earrings in her ears. I didn't think they were allowed to wear religious symbols. I mean to ask her about it but the opportunity hasn't presented itself.

The fourth person is my solicitor. Appointed by the state. I keep forgetting he's here. He's sitting right back in his chair, out of my eyeline, so when he leans forward to put his hand on my arm it startles me. Every time. He's urging caution. That's what his gesture means. I don't know his name either. I never knew it although he's told me twice. I didn't try to remember.

I yawn. I don't want them to think they're boring me, although they are, or that I'm disrespecting the process, but I can't help it. It's the lack of windows. And the closed door. The air doesn't move. We keep breathing the same air. It's been inside all of us many times by now.

'We won't keep you much longer.' It's the one who thinks I

killed her. 'There are just a few things we don't fully understand.'

I lean back in my chair. It's plastic. The chair. The type that flexes around you if you push hard against it. I keep doing that. It hurts. It digs into me. I am waiting for him to tell me what they are, the things he doesn't fully understand, but I realise he's not going to. He's writing again. Or still. Maybe he's forgotten he even said it. I listen for noises outside of the room. I can't hear anything. It seems nothing gets in or out. All I can hear is the tape recorder whirring away on the table.

'Do you want me to tell you it all from the start again?'

I'm pressing the phone hard to my ear to block out the noise. I can only just hear it ringing on the other side. There is a man seated at a counter nearby. I can only see half his face from this angle. There is more of it in the glass partition in front of him but I'm not looking. I close my eyes. To block out the noise. I can still hear it, but it's different now I can't see it. The phone is still ringing. It will go to voicemail shortly. I don't know what I should do when that happens. I try to imagine what sort of message I could leave. I hang up and dial again. I don't want to give up, although the prospect of someone answering terrifies me. It's just ringing. I can see it there, on the kitchen counter, on a small shelf in the hall, on a bedside table. I imagine I can. I've never been there. In their home. I hang up again. There is no one else I want to call.

Still here. Still going over the same old ground. Still saying the same things in different ways. I'm talking about Flo now. He wants to know all about her. About us. All the tiny, irrelevant details. I'm telling him how I ended up moving in next door, about going to the beach every morning, about her waiting for me on the stairs. Beside her pot plants. He smiles. I think he likes that image. But I'm wrong.

'Sorry,' he says, 'remind me who Flo is again?'

He knows who Flo is. I told him the first time. I've told him every subsequent time. I glare at him but he's not even looking. *Scratch, scratch, scratch* goes his pen over the paper. This is why it's taking so long. Questions like this. Deliberately obtuse. I wonder if he's got troubles at home and wants to drag this out so he doesn't have to go there. I look for a wedding ring. There isn't one. Maybe he's just trying to wear me down for some reason.

'She was the only person I spoke to in months,' I say. 'And the same for her. Do you know what co-dependent means?'

I tell him how I used to go around there every day, almost every day, and how saddened I was when she died. He wants to know how I knew she was deceased. What I did to confirm it. Did I wet a finger and hold it beneath her nose? Did I feel for a pulse? Or try to rouse her? Did I do anything at all?

'And you didn't call anyone, either. That's correct?'

I don't know what to say to this. I try to remember what I said the other times he's asked me this same question. He's asked it a lot. It's a particular sticking point for him. This must be one of those things he was talking about. That he doesn't fully understand. I don't blame him. I don't fully understand it either. I've tried to rationalise my actions – my inactions – since then but it's not easy. I tell him I was shocked to find her there. That I mean shocked in the medical sense, as in *in shock*, and that I think I was not ready to say goodbye. I tell him about co-dependence again, our odd version of it, and that I think that must have played a part in denying to myself that she'd really gone. At first at least. I say that when I was able to accept it, if I ever truly have, it seemed too late and that I'm not stupid and I knew how it would have looked by then. I'd used her phone. I'd used her credit card. Every day for weeks.

'I'm not certain about any of this,' I say. Or admit. 'It's just what I've deduced after the fact.'

He nods.

'You were motivated by money then.'

'I wasn't motivated by anything. I have my own money. From the house. I used her credit card because... I don't know why I used her credit card.'

He pages back in his notebook. Then forwards again. He is looking for something. Or pretending to. Some half-remembered detail that will unlock it all. He points to something written down and Chantal leans over to read it. She nods at him like she agrees, but he ignores her. He finds the next blank page and goes on writing again. I think he's playing games now. He thinks he's being clever, leaving me alone with my thoughts. Like that will coax out some new confession. *I know you're withholding something.* That's what his silence is saying to me. He's wrong though. I've told him everything.

'She was meant to be your friend.' He surprises me when he says this. After so long a pause.

'She was my friend.'

'I'd hate to know how you treat your enemies.'

'You know how I do. I've told you that also.'

The phone is back on my ear. But the room is quieter now. There is a hush. Most people have gone home. I don't have to press so hard to hear. I'm glad they're not answering. But I'm annoyed too. Where are they? They've gone out somewhere. Living their best life. I wonder if they've gone out together or alone. It's

Saturday. I stand up. It feels good to stretch my legs. The man at the counter turns to look at me. It's a different man to earlier. We stare at each other. I wonder what he knows about me. They must talk. He doesn't look away. Eventually I do. Or I close my eyes rather. It's not because I'm tired. I'm not. I've been awake I don't know how long, but I'm alert. It's the adrenaline. I listen to the phone still ringing. If a phone rings in an empty house, did it even ring at all? Maybe I'm more tired than I thought. I hang up again. Another let-off.

I've just realised something. Chantal is really Charmaine. That was Grace's friend. Charmaine. I look at her and try to change her name in my head. But it's too late. I can't do it. Chantal she is, and Chantal she will remain.

She's the one talking to me now. It's a welcome change. He's just sitting there writing in his book again. He doesn't look up. Not even once. She is not so young as I first thought. But she is still pretty, in a deceptive, understated sort of way. She has a sprinkle of freckles behind the silver crosses in her ears. Maybe it's the uniform I like. The promise of domination. Her manner is a bit like that too. She is far more authoritative than I ever expected her to be when she was playing the subordinate. I've warmed to her. She's talking to me about the Great White Hope now, about when he arrived and what happened when he did. She hasn't asked me who Flo is. I'm answering all her questions as fully as I can. I'm even trying to pre-empt her next question and answer that too. To save time. To make her life easier. To show him that a different approach provokes a different response.

'I'd urinated on myself,' I say. I don't want to say this to her, it's humiliating, but in the spirit of full disclosure and so forth.

'That's why he couldn't smell her. He could smell her. But he thought it was me.'

She doesn't react. It's to her credit. Maybe she likes that sort of thing. I could go off on a tangent very easily now. I tell her that she'd given me a key, Flo that is, after her fall, and that I gave it to him and then just waited for him to come back. I explain how angry he was. Not angry, but I don't know how else to explain it. Actors try to make the face he was making when something awful is meant to have happened in their film. I used to think they did it well until I saw that face for real. I tell her he started coming towards me and then stopped when he saw the ashtray in my hand.

'We were both surprised to see it there,' I say. 'I honestly have no idea when I picked it up.'

I'm on surer ground here. These are just the facts. There is no interpretation required. I tell her that even then I didn't know I was going to kill him, and that I was probably more stunned than he was when I bonked him on the head. That I wasn't even sure I'd done it because there was no blood. Not on the ashtray or on him. But then I saw the dent in his head. Just here.

I'm aware this is all quite disturbing, what I'm saying. But it's just words now. They've lost their meaning through constant repetition. I've said all this before. How he crawled about a bit on the floor. How he tried to get up. He did get up. How he began pulling himself along the wall towards the door but that I was by the door – I'd closed it by then – and that he saw me there and stopped moving towards it. How I hit him again. And again. I tell her that I'm sorry I just don't know how many times I hit him. She says it's not important. She smiles. I think it's a smile.

'The Queen of the Fairies is called Chantal,' I say. 'Are you also a queen?'

'My name isn't Chantal.'

There is a faint tap on my arm. It's my solicitor again. He is smiling gently at me. I look at the hand still on my arm, with its stubby fingers that belong with nicotine stains. I notice he's got a briefcase on his lap that he's not opened since we've been here. Maybe there's just a sandwich and an apple inside.

'You said he was angry and was coming towards you?'

'Yes. So?'

'You said you thought he was going to kill you?'

'Yes. So?'

'So I just wondered if it might not have been self-defence.'

The same man from earlier is still behind the desk. He's lost interest in me now though. He's sat back in his chair with his hands behind his head. There are sweat patches under his arms. They stand out against his white shirt. I pick up the phone and dial again. One or both of them will be in bed. I look around the walls. Why are there no clocks here either? I've not slept in so long. I can hear it ringing. I imagine it startling a sleeping house. Maybe someone is awake now, is walking groggily towards it. Bare feet on lush carpet.

'Hello?' A female voice, thick with sleep.

'Dolores?'

'Yes? Who is this please?'

'It's me.'

I listen to her thinking. She wants to hang up the phone. I want her to as well. I don't want to have to say it. She is next to me. She is laughing. I think I am laughing too. We're outside. The smell of cold air. Grace is there. I can't see her. She is the bundle I'm carrying and the stockinged feet over my shoulders. My hands encircle her ankles entirely.

'What do you want? Do you know what time it is?'

'Oh, Dolores. I've done something awful. Something truly awful.'

I am suddenly aware of how tired I am. It's hit me all at once. I feel light-headed. Light all over. When did I last eat anything? I want to sleep. But he is talking to me again. Questions beget questions. He's not even writing things down now. His notepad is gone. All his attention is on me.

'You so nearly got to France, didn't you? To your daughter. How long has it been since you've seen her?'

There is a brown folder on the table between us. I've just noticed it. I don't know where it came from. Or how long it's been there. No one has acknowledged it. I have a bad feeling.

'Do you want to know how we found you? Before you got there? A member of the public saw you. You walked right past them on the street. As if you didn't have a care in the world. But you were covered in blood. It was all over your face. Up your arms. Smeared on your shirt. They even took a picture and sent it to us. You had no idea? You're looking right into the camera. Now, as odd as that is, we only really paid attention when we got another call from someone else. They were only a few miles away, and they'd just found a body, beaten to death in a layby. Quite a thing. The great British public.'

1,991 days. That's how long it's been since I saw her. I'm not telling him that though. An image of my shoebox pops into my head. I want it. What have they done with it? I see him reading our letters. Laughing. I can feel my eyes wanting to close. I'm trying to fight it. My head feels heavy. He bangs the table with his flat hand. I look up. He is holding the folder towards me. I don't take it. He drops it on the table.

'There are a few photos we'd like you to take a look at.'

There is a new smell in the room. Mixed in with the stale air. Coffee and dried sweat. It's him. Chantal wouldn't be so uncouth. Chantal. I try to remember why I thought that was her name. There was a reason. It's gone. My head is hurting. I close my eyes again. Or they shut by themselves. If no one spoke for ten seconds I'd be asleep. Bang. He hits the table. Harder this time. He's staring at me. There is a thumbprint on the lens of his glasses. He doesn't seem to care. I care. If I had the energy I'd slap them off his face.

'Look,' he says.

He nods at the folder that's now right in front of me. I open it and there is a picture of Flo. Of Doris. She is alive. She is wearing a green cardigan. I recognise it. I close the folder.

'There's more,' he says.

After the green cardigan there are a few other photos of her. I don't know who took them. Derek, I assume. She is next to a Christmas tree. She is outside on the pavement. I look at the building behind her. It looks like where we used to live but there's not enough of it in the frame to be sure.

'Keep looking.'

I turn again. I gasp. I close the folder quickly. I look at my solicitor for help but he's not there. I fired him. I remember that now.

'You did that to her.'

'No.'

'Yes. Tell me why you killed her.'

'I didn't kill her.'

'Tell me how you killed her then.'

'I didn't.'

'You did.'

'I didn't. She was my friend.' I bunch up my fists and put them into my eyes. I want another pair of hands for my ears.

Someone in the room is breathing loudly. But I can still hear the machine whirring away on the desk. I miss her. I only think the words but I hear myself saying them. I am talking about them all. About Flo and Grace and even Dolores. What a mess I've made of everything.

'Look. Look at what you did to her. Your so-called friend.'

'I want my shoebox back.'

Chapter Thirty-Four
Then

Poor Reginald. He is officially still missing. After all this time. We never actually called off the search. The gaps between looking just got longer and longer. This last one has lasted years. There are still lamp-posts with bits of our posters stuck to them. White strips of paper under the Sellotape. The rest of it, with his picture and our number and the word 'missing', has gone. Like the dog himself. Poor Reggie. Poor me.

I used to talk to him. I miss that. It wasn't just *good boy* and *bad boy* and *walkies* and *dinner*. They were long talks. Not serious talks. It's not like I told him things I never did anyone else. But we chatted. I'd wake him up to have them. Often when the house was sleeping. I'd get down on the rug next to him and slide my hand under his head and then put my head right on his. Cheek to snout. I'd start saying his name over and over. The poor beast would be fast asleep at first. But then his tail would stir, it would lift and flop down in a single, groggy sign that he was waking up and that he was happy to be waking up to my voice. 'Here he comes,' I'd say, with a smile in my voice. His tail would go again. His breathing would change. An eye would open. It would be red. Full of gunge. A browny-grey gunk that pasted his eyelashes together or gathered in a sticky ball in the corner. He'd just lay there at first, giving me the side-eye. But his tail gave him away. What I liked most was when our faces were side by side, cheek to snout, and we were both gently pressing together. To stay close. I could feel him pressing against me. I'd tell him to lie down again, that I wasn't going anywhere, then I'd roll over and put my head on his belly and stroke his chest, in the furry vulnerable bit between his front legs. I'd sometimes get this horrific thought of someone, maybe even me, sticking something long and thin – a knitting needle or a straightened out coat-hanger – into that part of him.

'Should I burn it down? When he's the only one in there? I think I could get away with it. He always stays later than everyone else. Like he's showing off even when there's no one there to show off for. I could put a wooden beam across the door. The fire would burn up the evidence. What do you think, Reggie?' This was before I quit. I was talking about Jason. I thought I was odd having these thoughts, but I've since discovered it's not so unusual. More than half of employees think about murdering their employer. It's quite normal. Even healthy. It turns them into real people and enables us to empathise with them better. That's the theory. I have to say, that wasn't my experience. Reggie would eventually go back to sleep. While I was still there. Still talking. I didn't mind. He snored. I used to love listening to it. He sounded like a human when he did it. Like a small child or an old man. It soothed me.

'*I don't understand how he could just disappear. He'll be so hungry.*'

'*Don't worry, he'll turn up. He'll turn up.*'

'*You've lost our dog. You've actually lost him.*'

I hadn't. I knew where he was the whole time.

That day. In the fields. I see it all unfold again. Exactly as it did. I hear the car engine turn off. I hear my door open and my boots hit the gravel. I hear Reggie barking. Already his barking is growing distant. He is off. He knows the way by now. I hear my car door closing and my footsteps crossing the small car park and then how the sound changes as I move onto the trail. I hear my breathing. I'm walking fast. I'm eager to get to where I'm going. The drugs are in my pocket. Every now and then I put my hand inside to make sure. Yes. Still there. And there's the lighter. And there's the second one. The reserve. The previous week I got to where I was going and the lighter didn't work. I tried it a thousand times. I screamed. I broke things. I had to retrace my steps and start the whole thing again. Every now and then I call his name. Sometimes he barks in reply. Sometimes he's far away but other times he surprises me by how close he is. It is windy. I notice that. It sweeps over the fields and makes the stalks move. They change colours as they lean one way then another. Moving all together. It's like a watching a swarm.

I want to get to the ditch. Where the broken tree trunk is. It's where I always go now. I'm eager to get there. I can hunker down out of the wind. It's not far. Maybe a mile. If that. My pace quickens. I hear my breath getting faster.

What I love about this time is that it's completely my own. Everyone I know thinks I'm somewhere else. Occupied by someone else. It's like a cross-stitch of alibis. I used to get up at about 3am sometimes. Just to be alone. Just to have a waking hour or two when someone wasn't there, picking at me, wanting something from me, taking something from me. But now I have this time. I have chiselled it out of thin air. It's all mine. If you want something badly enough, then go and get it. Make it happen.

I am here now. I stand above the ditch looking around me. I am nowhere at all. In each direction the fields roll away into the distance. The only buildings I can see are far off. They are hazy and shapeless. They can't touch me here. I look up at the branch. The same branch I always look at. The robin is there. I'm infatuated with him. Seeing him there, it makes me think everything is right with the world. We're all exactly where we're meant to be today. He chirps his hello. He hops one step sideways. To get a better view of me. I'm certain of it. Unobstructed by leaves. His tiny head twitches to the side. Chirp, chirp. That's me. Greeting him back. I'm close to tears.

Reggie is here now. He is sniffing at something in the ditch. Perhaps I left crumbs last time. I jump down there to join him. 'What's up, beast?' I rub him under his chin. He looks up at me and smiles. I squat down in front of him. I'm holding his head in my hands, looking at him gravely. 'I do love you, my friend. You understand what I'm saying.' I hug him. With my face buried in his coat. I am crying now. He lets me hold him a moment. He stands there patiently. He's humouring me. He knows all this. He loves me back. But he's eager to be off. I let him go. I try to pat his side before he runs off but he's too quick and it's barely a glancing blow. I call him back. I want to give him a proper stroke. But he's gone. That faint fingertip brush down his side, it will have to do.

I sit down on the wood and begin to smoke. I lean back against the dry mud wall. It's hard and caked so it won't leave a mark. I could be in the trenches. I imagine the exposed roots to be the limbs of half-buried soldiers. I close my eyes. I keep smoking. I feel the ash land on my wrist. I let it. A gust will take it when it's good and ready. I am overwhelmed by how much I love this solitude. It's not love. It's need. Everything was so fast and chaotic. It was making my bones rattle. But not out here. Out here I can breathe at my own speed. If I want to contemplate – I don't, but if I did – I've got the time and space to do it.

I wonder if I should bring Dolores one day. When it's all out in the open. Would it be better? The sudden knot in my stomach tells me it wouldn't. But no one could see us here. Under the sky. Maybe she'd be prepared to get her knees dirty. I feel a stirring. I consider acting on it. But even if she did I'd resent her presence the minute I'd finished. No. Better alone.

Reggie is back. He puts his wet nose against my cheek. I smile. Then he's gone again. Good for him. Good for you. This is your special time, too. You enjoy it. I say this. Or think it. It doesn't matter. He's no longer here to hear me. I will bring Dolores. I mustn't be so mean to her. We can be friends again. She has my best interests at heart. I'd do well to remember that. My head is tipping forward. I let it. I like this feeling of gravity, of slouching fully forward and being absorbed into the earth. I'm debris at the bottom of the ditch. I can hear the wind but I can't feel it. Not down here. It can't get me down here. It roars over the land like a locomotive. Or maybe that was a locomotive. We're not too far from the tracks. I'm nearly asleep.

'You've actually lost our dog.'
　'Don't worry. He'll turn up.'

I am cold and my body is aching. I am getting to my feet. I'm not sure how long I was asleep. Maybe I wasn't asleep. I feel like I was. Like my body is doing things but my mind is a step behind. It could be ten minutes later or two hours. I don't know the time. I look up. There are clouds so I can't see the sun to even make a guess. I call Reggie. I bend down to pick up the lighter that I must have dropped. I look around for anything else. Any other sign of me. I feel the chocolate wrappers in my pocket. Or hear them rather. When I rub my pocket through my jeans.

Balancing on the trunk is the water bottle. It's empty. How? I call Reggie.

It's easier getting into the ditch than it is getting out. I need both hands. I have to hold on to things and heave myself up. It takes some effort. Once I'm out I bend over with my hands on my knees to gather my breath. Reggie usually barrels into me at this point. I turn my hanging head left and right and look at the upside-down world. I can't see him. Carefully, giving the blood time to move with me, I stand up. I notice that the robin has gone. The empty branch looks lost without it. For no reason at all I take it as a sign of foreboding.

I begin walking back the way I came. The way we came. He'll find me. He'll catch my scent and come bounding after me. He knows the way. Sometimes he's even been back at the car waiting for me. I keep walking. I keep calling. I keep looking behind me. He's not at the car. When I get there. I knew he wouldn't be. But I walked all the way anyway. Just to make sure. I unload my pockets and the empty water bottle and then set off back towards the ditch. I am aware my pulse is quickening now. Not from the walking. Our bodies are fine things. Instinctual. They sense danger before our ever so logical brains do. I'm more than halfway back. I stop and call his name. I close my eyes to listen better. Sometimes you could hear him even when you couldn't see him. Rustling among the stalks. He sounded different from the wind. But I don't hear him in the fields. I keep listening. Another sound is rushing up on me. It is getting louder and louder. It's right on top of me. It whooshes past me and then begins to fade. I open my eyes again. The train is already off in the distance. Heading back to town. I watch it until I can't see it anymore.

I start to sob. I don't know why. I try to convince myself that I don't know why. I clench my teeth to stop myself, to get a grip, but the opposite happens and I can't hold it back anymore and suddenly everything just pours out of me and first I bend over double and then I crumple completely and I'm on my hands and knees hitting the ground with my fists while snot streams out of my nose and I don't even care because I've not bawled like this since I was five.

Eventually I stand up again. 'Reggie? Reggie?' I say his name this time. Conversational tone. I don't bother calling. I know. I don't know how I know. It doesn't matter. The robin wasn't there. That's how I know. What does that mean? A stupid bird. Who cares how? But I know. I leave the path and begin walking directly towards the tracks.

There is a small verge leading up to them. I walk up it and balance on one of the rails. The only thing I don't know is which way I should walk. I decide to go left. Away from the town. Towards my ditch. As I walk I'm scanning in front of me. I'm not sure exactly where I should be looking. On the track, at the bottom of the verge, in the ribbon of clear ground before where the fields start, or in the fields themselves. I keep walking. I don't call his name anymore. I pass my ditch. I walk further. Five minutes. Ten minutes. Then turn around. I keep scanning, in case I missed something the first time. But there is nothing. I should be getting hopeful. I'm not. I know I'll find him sooner or later. I pass my ditch again. I reach the point where I emerged onto the tracks and I keep going. The line bends slightly. I can't see around the corner. I walk around it. I expect to see him at any moment. But I don't. There is movement in the bushes. Something brown is in there. Reggie is brown. I stand and wait. A hare sticks his head out then darts across the track and disappears. I continue walking.

When I finally see him I'm not shocked. It is only confirmation of what I already knew. He is about fifty yards in front of me. At the bottom of the verge. From where I am I can tell that he's been split open. I look down at my feet. I decide I won't look at him properly again. I step down from the track and walk along the verge. The ground is easier here. I am looking down the whole time. When I see him at the top of my vision I stop and turn around. I look for a stick. A hard one. I find a bit of old track instead. It's flat. Like a paddle. It will do perfectly. I begin to dig. I expect to find myself scratching my way through a rough layer of stone and gravel and other obstinate minerals. But the ground gives way easily and in no time at all I'm able to discard the piece of track and scoop out the earth with my hands. I'm not sure how deep to make it. I jump into the hole. It's past my knees. I decide that will do. I climb out and back up to where Reggie is lying. I still won't look. I put a hand out behind me, feeling tentatively along the ground until my fingers touch a paw. I drag it towards the grave. I won't look. I step over the hole I've dug. The weight on the end of my arm changes as he slides over the edge. I lean forward and like a dog myself I begin shovelling dirt backwards between my legs. When I'm satisfied I stand up and walk away. I don't look back.

Rather than deal with this I decide that it didn't happen. None of it. This must be why I didn't look at him. I've never been here before. I reach the car. I am driving. I am at home. Reggie isn't here. His basket is empty. I fill up his bowl and call him. He doesn't come. I open the front door and call him. He doesn't come. I wonder where he is. This isn't like him at all. I hope he turns up soon. He was here and then he was gone. I just don't understand it. We'll make posters and stick them up all over town.

Chapter Thirty-Five
Now

I am in the dock. What a peculiar thing to say about oneself. And for it to be true. Literally true. Not in the metaphorical sense. Which is how it's meant nine times out of ten. But not this time. I am literally standing in the dock. I am in a brown suit. It's not mine. They gave it to me. I'd never wear brown voluntarily.

The judge is talking now. He has been talking for ages. That's because he's repeating the same thing but with different words. *Despicable, shameful, reprehensible.* He's called me all these things. He's hamming it up. That's what's going on here. He's in love with the sound of his own voice. I can tell. His neck has gone red with excitement. His fat lips are wet. He's positively salivating. I bet his little willy – and it will be little – is twitching beneath his gown.

Every now and then I glance behind me and scan the faces in the courtroom. There aren't many people here. Every one of them is a stranger. Good. I'm just checking. Just making sure that they've not snuck in behind my back. Dolores and Grace, I mean. I ordered them not to come. Dolores said I needn't worry about that. She said she had no intention of coming. And that Grace would only be here over her dead body.

'But that's not a phrase I can use now, is it?'

'Are you picking a fight with me, Dee? Really? Even now?'

She hung up.

The judge has an ugly face. It is big and loose and it wobbles when he talks. Even when he's stopped talking. He had acne once. I can see the craters it's dug into his skin. You never get rid of it. Not completely. All that pus and poison will still be there, just seething beneath the surface, waiting for a chance to erupt again. I bet if I stuck a fingertip really hard into one part of his face then another part would start to ooze. I'm being nasty, of course. It's nothing personal. It's just that he's the one who is going to decide the rest of my life for me. That's why we're all here. That's why I'm staring. Hoping to shove his verdict back down his throat. I've been told I should expect something in the region of twenty-five years. I've been told it would have been over thirty had I not pleaded guilty as soon as I did. That's not why I did it. I wasn't thinking about any of that. I just think when you carry something so big, you have to share it eventually. It has to do with being other. Of not wanting to be. Secrets isolate us.

There is a noise behind me and I turn around again. It's not them. I realise that I may never see them again. My family. So-called. I realise that I don't care all that much. I have started blaming them for my predicament. I know I did the deed. But they did nothing to discourage me. It could be argued their actions even encouraged me. I see Dolores at the front door – my front door – ushering me out of it. Closing it even before I am off the porch. I see Grace hunched over her desk, composing that last letter she wrote me, accusing me of leaving her as well as her mother, and of not loving her. How could she think such a thing? I've said before how carelessly cruel children can be to their old folk. And yet. And yet I wonder if she may not be right. I always just took it for granted that I loved them. Both of them. And that I always would. I just assumed it to be true. But I think now that I could learn to hate them. That I'm already learning to. I wonder where I'll be then? Because if I don't have them who do I have? But it's true about love and hate being two sides of the same coin. It's Day 2,003. I don't give a fuck.

'Your actions offend the sensibilities of all right-thinking people.'

And still he goes on. The judge. Perhaps this is my sentence. Listening to him drone on until he or I drop down dead. I look at his swollen lips flapping open and shut. Someone will have kissed those lips. Someone maybe still does. Now that is despicable, shameful, the other thing he said. I kick the rail in front of me. The sudden noise interrupts him. He pauses. He glances at me. He starts up again. I have an urge. I wonder how close I could get. If I leaped over the rail and charged. There are two policemen in the court today. They are as far from me as they are from him. The element of surprise would work in my favour.

'You have committed a wicked series of offences and inflicted unfathomable, unprovoked brutality. Your crimes are heinous in the extreme and can only be those of a depraved, deeply disturbed human being.'

I said I was sorry. What more does he want? 'I'm sorry,' I said. When I was invited to say a few words. This was after the prosecution spoke and before the judge took over. The judge looked at me for a long while. He seemed unimpressed. Like I was being irreverent somehow. I think when people like me annoy him he must imagine we're the ones who teased him about his spots. He wanted to know if that was all I had to say for myself? *All*, I thought? *All? Isn't sorry meant to be the hardest word?* I shrugged at him. 'I'm very sorry then.'

He is winding up now. At last. He is going through the list one final time. Murder. Guilty. Fraud by false representation. Guilty. Preventing lawful burial. I didn't even know that was a crime. Breaking and entering. I shake my head. It bothers me that they think I'm guilty of this too. It means they don't believe we were ever friends.

A door closes somewhere. I look back again. There is no one new in the court room. It was only someone leaving.

Twenty-two years. That's my sentence. He's just said it. Life, obviously, all murder is life. But without parole for at least twenty-two years. That's the bit that matters. He's looking at me for a reaction. I have nothing for him. I am not happy. Not unhappy. It is just a fact. I'm not required to feel anything about it. I stare back dispassionately. Without further ceremony he rises and sweeps out of the court room. I watch his gown billowing behind him. Everyone else is on their feet too. And Grace is among them. I see her now. She is picking her way between a row of seats. I knew she'd come. I knew she'd not abandon me. At my bewitching hour. She was here all the time. A firm hand lands on my shoulder. It begins steering me out of the dock. I look past the body it's attached to. I am elated that she's here. It's reassured me no end. I lied about nearly hating her. How could I ever? I couldn't.

'Grace!'

She is taller than she was. And thinner. She is walking towards the exit at the back of the courtroom.

'Grace!'

She turns. It's not her. She is much older. She is pretty. I stare at a woman I don't know. She stares back. I'm nudged from behind. Through a doorway. The door closes and she's gone. I forget her almost immediately.

Chapter Thirty-Six
Now

I am in a holding cell beneath the court. Someone calling himself The Insider is talking to me. He is telling me what it will be like. What I should expect. The first day. The first week. Beyond that. He is standing far too close. I can see the tattoo on the inside of his forearm. It's a date. Three years ago. There is a name there too. I realise he's a father. Just like me. I refuse to believe I'm in the same category as him.

I should be relieved. That's what I've been told. About the twenty-two years. I've been told it is a let-off. There was certainly a murmur in the courtroom. When he said it. I saw it on their faces too. Not outrage. Not quite. Resentment though, certainly. I don't feel relieved. I thought I would. I thought clarity and closure would clear my head. Calm me down. I am not becalmed. I am more agitated than ever. The Insider is right in my face. He doesn't mean to be confrontational. He is just excited. He's talking too fast. Starting one sentence before finishing the last. I hate people who do that. Like they're too important, too busy, to say the extra few words. I realise he's boasting. He's enjoying being the expert. For once in his life. He pats my arm. He is my buddy. He thinks he is. He couldn't be more wrong. I push him against the wall. An officer – he's not a police officer – grabs my shoulders and slams me down onto the bench. He holds me down there. The Insider is staring at me. He looks affronted.

'Let's get one thing straight,' I say. 'We're not the same, you and I.'

A van door slides open. I'm shoved inside, along a narrow alley and into an empty cubicle. It looks like the inside of a festival toilet, but I'm the nasty deposit here. The door shuts behind me and after a moment the engine starts. I wonder who else is in here. In the other cubicles. I saw faces in glass. I wonder how thick the walls are and if I talk whether they would hear me. I want to ask them about drowning. It's the least of my worries now, I know that, but the thought is there. The van is designed this way for security reasons. I understand that. But what if we swerve off a bridge and into a river? The driver would have to swim outside the vehicle to reach us. Would he remember which key to use? Would the door even open underwater? He'd just swim away. I know he would. That's what I'd do.

I can hear someone shouting through the partition. They are kicking it. It's coming from behind me and in front of me. I feel like it's intended for me. I stare out the tiny window. I keep looking for windows now, and out of them. It's because on the other side is a world I'm not part of anymore. More shouting. More banging. I don't make a sound. I need the toilet. I don't know how far we're going. I didn't ask.

Attitude. That's what The Insider said. Maybe I was listening. He said it was my best survival tool. And I needed to get it right. If I was too weak I'd be used. *Used.* His word. It doesn't bear thinking about. But if I was too tough – no chance of that – I'd very quickly meet someone tougher. And I didn't want that.

They have stopped shouting now. And kicking. I keep staring out of the small box window. I still need the toilet. I hold it, the tip of it, but I can feel it swelling like a long balloon. Lights from cars coming the other way sweep through my cubicle. When did it get so dark? All those cars. They are all heading into my past, going to where I've been. I want to go with them.

Someone behind me starts barking. It startles me and a squirt of urine comes out. I cross my legs. He keeps doing it. He sounds like an angry dog behind a gate. Reggie didn't sound like that, but other dogs do. I can't hold it in any longer. I push my face into the side as my bladder empties.

I'm half naked now. The floor is cold on my bare feet. I am told to hold myself in my hands and turn all the way around. So they can have a good look. I feel like a specimen. I'm told to get dressed. Only I don't have my clothes anymore. I have their clothes. Their jogging bottoms and their sterile T-shirt. The same as everyone else. Even the pants and socks are theirs. I say my name silently to myself while I put them on. *Self. Identity. Self. Identity.* I'm taken to a chair. A contraption rather. 'Sit there.' He tells me it's called The BOSS. I don't understand. He says it's The BOSS because when I sit in it, I'll realise I'm not the boss anymore. BOSS stands for Body Orifice Security Scanner. But I don't know that yet.

I sign forms. So many forms. What if I didn't sign them? What if I refused? I've not read any of them. I have my photo taken. I am paraded in front of people I don't know. The medical team, the probation officer, the prison warden. I like the prison warden though. When he looks at me, he smiles. He doesn't smile at the others like that. I check. I think he suspects that I am out of place here. That I don't really belong. He's right. I don't. I plan to develop a personal rapport with him.

'You're stuck here,' he says, to all of us, but mainly to me I think, 'so you might as well make the best of it. Now go on.'

In front of me is my cell. The door is open. It's waiting for me. I stop walking and the guard puts his hand gently on the small of my back.

'This is you,' he says.

Something hits me. It's the sudden knowledge that I am the monster the judge described. That I am him. I grab the bars to stop myself falling over.

'It will be fine.' The guard's hand presses softly against my back. 'Everyone is like this their first night.'

I must ask him a question. To delay it. Think. Think. He closes the door and I hear the bolt lock. His footsteps get quieter and quieter. Then I can't hear them at all. In front of me is a bed, a sink, a toilet. A small television set on the wall. It's exactly like the last prison was. During the trial. Only it's much worse somehow. I walk over and sit on the bed. There is a call button too. They said I can press it if I want to speak to someone. A Listener. That's what they called them. Samaritan-trained. What would I say? I'm sorry. I'm very sorry. I said that already. I look down. The parcel they gave me is still in my hands. Inside it are a few biscuits – the type Flo had when it was just the two of us, but it was always just the two of us – and a carton of orange juice. It's because I missed dinner. That's why they gave it to me. I'll be here for breakfast though. The thought makes me queasy. I throw the parcel against the wall. It explodes and some of the contents bounce back and hit me. That's how small the room is. It's not a room. It's a cell.

I'm standing up in the boardroom. *Sit down*. People are looking. *Sit down*. My brogues are squeaking across the varnished floorboards. I'm at the door. I'm off. I hear myself say it. I'm going to be a pilot. *You idiot*. I'm brushing past Dolores at our front door. Not hers. Not mine. It was ours. I'm walking down the path. I'm not stopping. *You stupid fucking idiot*.

I'm at a loss. I look at the call button. I pull the blanket back. Jesus. I can't sleep on that. What do I do now, Flo? Around me on the wing are all the other prisoners. I can't see them, but they're there, and I will know them soon. I will eat with them and shower with them and spend half my life again with them. I am one of them now.

The lights go out and we're all plunged into darkness. The barking starts again. It's the same barking. The same person. I put my hands to my cheeks. I think that juice got in my eyes. When the carton burst open. It's made them water.

Chapter Thirty-Seven
Then

I put my head in the doorway. Flo is where she always is. I can see the top of her head above the back of the chair. 'Knock, knock,' I say. 'Hello.' She half turns. Not all the way. She raises a hand in greeting. I walk in and sit next to her. She nods at the window. That is the way she acknowledges me now. Anything more is too much effort. It's the stroke. She's not been the same since then. She keeps saying the same word to me. Only half her mouth moves so I couldn't work it out at first. Incapacitated. That's what she's saying to me. It's a difficult word to say at the best of times. I pat her hand. 'I know,' I say, 'I know.' She does turn her head now and glares at me. She's angry. There is fury inside of her, shining out of her eyes. She's furious about her situation, her condition, and she's furious with me too. I look away quickly. At the boats. There are no boats. At the place where the boats would be. Anywhere but at her. I know what her look is saying to me. Demanding of me.

'You're letting me down.'

I get up and make us both a cup of tea. I know she won't drink hers. What she will sip at she'll spill down herself. It's just something for me to do. I sit back down. It's a cold day but the sun is out. I watch it moving across the sky. Now and then clouds pass in front of it and an ominous shadow rushes up the sand towards us. It's just a shadow. I say ominous only because of the atmosphere. It's been getting closer. This day. We both know it. I sip my tea. It's stone cold. As I put the cup down I take the opportunity to steal a look at her. She's still awake, but only just. Her eyelids are half closed. She's fighting it. I want to stroke her head. To look deep, deep into her eyes and tell her it will all be okay. I want her to say the same to me. Because this is happening to both of us. We've both been waiting for it.

There are boats now. Or a boat. A single trawler floating above the swells. I wish for an instant to be on it. To be any of those fishermen instead of myself. But I was never made for the sea. I still don't know why I ended up living beside it, right here. Maybe for this very moment. I am listening to her breathe. It's not a snore. Not yet. It's on the way to becoming a snore. I look again at her. Her mouth is hanging a fraction open. There is a string of spit between her lips. It moves in and out with her breath. Okay. Enough time has passed now.

I get up and go to the bed. It's a double bed, with two pillows on each side. I wonder which side is Len's and which is hers. It will still be that way. These things don't change. I pick up the pillow nearest to me. It's soft and light. Some pillows are heavier, but this one feels perfect. I press it over my face for a few moments. I try to breathe while I'm doing it. I keep pressing harder until I can't breathe. I look at Flo. She's not moved. I've never done this before. I wonder how it will change me. I walk towards her and without hesitating for a second I lean over the back of the chair and put the pillow over her face. She doesn't move, doesn't even twitch. I expected some sort of physical response, but there is nothing at all. I'm holding my breath. Like I do under water. So I can gauge the time. I hold it longer than I ever have before, longer than I even thought I could. She still hasn't moved. I'm hoping she has just passed straight from sleep. My arms are shaking now. I can't keep applying the same pressure to the pillow but also I don't want to take it away yet. I lean right over and hold it in place with my body while I hug her towards me. I keep reminding myself that this is what she wants. That she's asked me for it day after day.

Incapacitated. Her word.

'I thought you were my friend,' she said. Tried to say. 'I'd do it for you.'

I take the pillow away and stand up. For a few moments I don't move. I'm holding my breath again and listening for hers. But I can't hear anything. A car passes beneath the window. I listen to it fade out of earshot and then I listen intently to the complete silence in the room. It's over. I'm someone different now.

I walk to the bed and put the pillow back where it was. What now? I sit down. It's a high bed and I have to turn my back on it and do a little backwards jump to get up here. My feet don't touch the floor. They dangle above it.

I look at Flo. At the bit of her head that I can see from here. Her hair is thin. I can see right through it to her scalp, where there is a wart, bright pink against the pale, almost fluorescent white of her skin. The wart is all bunched at the top, like it's being drawn down a hole in the middle. I think irreverently of a baboon's arse. I get a sudden urge to walk up behind her and squeeze it.

'What should I do now?' I ask her. 'Come on, this was your bright idea.'

I hop off the bed and return to the chair. I lean across, so my face is right in front of hers. I'm looking for something to be different in her. But she looks just as she did when she was falling asleep. In some way I'm fascinated. I prod her arm. I prod it harder. I almost shove her. All she does is tilt. I study her face. I can see the day reflected in bulbous miniature in her eyes. They're open now. They weren't. I decide not to think about that. Something flashes across them. A bird perhaps. I reach across and close the lids with the tips of my thumb and index finger, the way I've seen people do it in the movies.

And that's that. I did it. I wasn't sure I would. Even as I was doing it. But once I started it got easier. Turns out starting was the hardest part. A lot of things are like that, I think.

I sit back in my chair and consider the scene. There are no signs there either, of what has just happened. There are clouds massing on the horizon. It is probably raining there. Or it soon will be. I can see tankers out there too. I can see their lights twinkling in the gloom. Nearer shore, the trawler has gone. The fishermen will be back in port, counting their catch or heading home for their tea. My stomach gurgles. I pat it. I remember that there was a flyer beneath the phone.

Chapter Thirty-Eight
Now

E very morning I do my exercises. Once I realise where I am. It still takes me a few moments to orientate myself. It shouldn't do. I've been here long enough. But I still wake up – sometimes, not every time – in a state of blank bewilderment. On these mornings I lie perfectly still. Reluctant to move my head even an inch off the pillow. I stare up at the ceiling. As if seeing it for the first time. I stare at the window, at the wall. It's when I stare at the wall that it all comes back to me. When I see the pieces of paper stuck to it. But I recognise that handwriting, I think. And then, ah, yes, I remember now. How could I forget?

I don't always do my exercises immediately. It depends on the time, on what I imagine the time to be. I'm able to guess it quite accurately now. That's because I've got to know the sounds around here, of the building, of the other prisoners I can't see, and the smells. Doors unlock at 8am. If it's early enough I'll put my hand inside my jogging bottoms. I like to imagine that Dolores is here, telling me to put on a show for her. She is standing beside the bed, looking down her nose at me. Her red hair is hanging on her shoulders. Maybe she is in her sheer blouse and pencil skirt again. Maybe she was but isn't anymore. Maybe I reach out a hand to touch her and she slaps it away playfully.

Please?

No. I know what those hands have done.

I'm still coming to terms with all that. It's like a bonfire in my path. I approach it slowly but can't ever get too close before I have to back away again. Somehow, I have to get around it before I can go on.

There is a scheme here called Restorative Justice. It involves talking to people affected by crimes similar to your own. My probation officer has put me on it. He thinks it will help me appreciate what I've done. Appreciate. I thought that was an odd choice of word. I sat with a woman yesterday. She told me all about her dead husband. Dead is somewhat evasive. Murdered. I was told that he was a good man. Selfless and kind and loving and etc, etc. When aren't they all these things? The deceased, I mean? You never hear a bad word about them. Just once I'd like to hear someone say, 'I never got on with him. He was a bit of an arse, to be honest.' But no, they're all saints apparently. Like God or whatever only wants the very best of us. I don't believe it. It's more random than that. Fate doesn't discriminate. He was thirty-seven when it happened. Her husband. She didn't say how it happened. She told me – I say me, there was a group of us, only I felt like she was talking only to me – she told me there were three children. Four, six and eleven. I wasn't sure if she meant that was how old they were at the time, or if that's how old they are now. She wasn't clear. She stopped talking then and stared at me, gauging my reaction.

I looked at my hands. It was a tragic tale. The poor kids. I felt like I should say something consoling. Something the probation officer would have approved of. But in the back of my head all I could hear was a sarcastic little voice. 'And?' it said. 'So what?'

It wasn't because I was unsympathetic towards Sarah. That was her name. Sarah. She was wearing a necklace outside her jumper with a silver S dangling from it. But I was thinking, I don't know this woman. Or her kids. I never met her husband and had no part in his demise. I couldn't work out why she was she making her problems mine. Yes, it was a sad story. But there are a million sad stories. Must our hearts break for each of them? I'm old school. Look after your own. That's what I always say. Do you hear me, Derek? None of this needed to happen. I kept looking at my hands. My nails needed cutting. One nail in particular. It kept scratching the adjacent fingertip. As soon as I became aware of it I had to stop listening to her and concentrate on not biting it.

'I wish the man who killed him was dead.'

This was much later in our talk. Near the end of our conversation. I'd managed to pick the loose nail free. I looked up then. She was staring at me. To make sure I knew how much she hated me. She was nearly crying. Or she had just finished. It was from the sadness and frustration and anger. But mostly the anger.

'I bet there are people who wish some of you were dead, too.'

'How is that helpful?' I asked.

She shook her head. She told me that I had misunderstood. That she wasn't there to help me. That was confusing because I thought she was. I thought that was the point. But maybe she had been at the start. She said why would she want to help people like me? People like me just contaminate. She told me that we're like black ink leaking into a jug of clear water, and that we could spend the rest of our lives repenting but the water in that jug would always be black now. I thought that was a good analogy. Very visual.

'The people who love you are in that jug, too,' she said.

.   .   .

My hand is still inside my jogging bottoms, but it's not really working this morning. My mind is elsewhere. What I'm holding flaps and folds between my fingers. I persevere a bit longer. Dolores. Pencil skirt. Sheer blouse. No. My heart's not in it. My arm is aching.

I get out of bed and take off my clothes. I fold them neatly and put them under the pillow. Then I begin star jumps. This is the start of my exercise routine. It's the same every day. I do 200 of them. It's easy. It's not a test. It's just to loosen me up, to get the blood flowing. I do them properly though. Rigid arms. Snapping them up and down in time with my feet and my breath. I stare at the same spot on the wall.

Immediately after the 200th one I fall forwards onto my palms and start doing press-ups. The transformation is one fluid movement. You can cheat doing press-ups. You can stick your arse in the air. You can only go a little way down. I don't cheat. I'd only be cheating myself. I go all the way down. So the tip of my nose and cock touch the floor at the same time. If they don't, then I don't count it. I can do 200 now. I think that's something to be proud of. When I started I couldn't even manage twenty. I thought fifty would be a landmark. But now I'm up to 200. That's an achievement, I think. At my age.

No one has come to see me here. Not once. That's my doing. I won't put their names on the visitor list. She's asked. I refuse. This is my penance. We still write.

From press-ups I flip straight over into the sit-up position. It's not possible to do proper sit-ups on a hard floor. I do crunches instead. They're just as effective. More so, if you do them correctly. Which I do. That means not using your explosive strength. But rolling your shoulders off the ground slowly, in a controlled manner, so each sit-up feels like the first. Even doing it this way hurts my back. My lower vertebrae. They're constantly bruised. I can feel the skin pinch with every up and down. Another 200.

Today is Day 3,000. Grace is seventeen. It was her birthday last week.

Then I'm back on my feet. High-stepping. It's easy to cheat at this too. You can lean back. Or not lift your knees high enough. But again, I don't cheat. Then it's squats, lunges, triceps dips, burpees. The same routine every morning. I think I'd come apart if I missed it just once. Or if I did 199 instead of 200. My final exercise is planking. The world record is more than eight hours. When I read that I didn't believe it. I had to find a second source to confirm it. I do maybe ten minutes. I don't measure planking in time, but by the drops of sweat that run off the end of my nose. I won't stop until I've counted fifty of them. Usually by then my whole body is trembling. It's trembling now. It's shaking. I'm pushing it past where it wants to be. I like this feeling. Fighting against myself. Refusing to listen to what my muscles are saying. I'm in control. Not you. Drip, drip, drip. Forty-three, forty-four, forty-five. I like the immediacy of pain. The urgency of it. I like how it consumes you. How it takes you over and stops you thinking about anything else. Forty-six, forty-seven, forty-eight. Drip, drip, drip. Because it's possible to overthink. Especially in here. With all this time. I'm constantly guarding against that. Forty-nine. The Devil makes work for idle minds. Fifty.

I stand up and dip my bald head under the cold tap. The water streams unobstructed down my back and chest. I try to concentrate on every bead as it rolls down my skin. I'm not allowed to wipe any of them away. This is also an exercise of control. Mind over body. I can hear noises outside my cell now. Other people. Television sets. Further away the tinny sound of metal on metal. I sit back down on the bed. I look at my cock and consider having another go. I can't be bothered. They put something in the food here.

Chapter Thirty-Nine
Now

My four walls are covered with letters. That's what the pieces of paper are. When they fall off or when a corner flaps away I pick off the Blu Tack, mould it into a neat ball again and then press the paper back down. They are the letters that were in the shoebox, plus all the letters she's written me since. I've arranged them in order. Left to right. Top to bottom. So I can read them like a story. That's often how they seem to me. Just as illusory. Sometimes I read them all. Sometimes, if I don't have much time, I just pick out parts. When I do this, I seem to read the same parts each time.

I'm married now, Daddy. I know I said I'd never get married. That I've only ever seen it turn out badly. But what we have is special. I suppose everyone thinks that at the start. But he is a good man. He has never lied to me. And you know how I value total honesty now. I think you'd like him. A few people have told me that he looks like you, but I don't see it at all. Although he is silly like you were. Are you still? It doesn't show in your letters if you are. But a Frenchman with a sense of humour. Who'd have believed it? I've included a few wedding photos with this letter. I hope you like them. Don't I look happy? That's because I am. It's not always been easy. I've had some very dark days, but Pierre has been so patient and understanding. It was a magical day, even with the rain. I wish you had been there. Pierre's father walked me down the aisle. It was good of him, but it made me sad. And you shouldn't feel sad on your wedding day.

Mummy has gone now. I think she tried to hold on to meet her first grandchild, but she was in too much pain and another three months was just too difficult for her. It really was frightening how quickly it happened. Only last year we were planning our once-in-a-lifetime holiday. It turns out it wasn't even that. I was there at the end. It was just the two of us. She was so brave. It sounds dreadful but I was relieved when she passed. For her. I know she's better off where she is. I wish you had let her speak to you at the end.

Pierre thinks that we should tell him about you now. I understand what he's saying. And I should be the last one wishing to keep secrets. He has asked where his grandparents are. Not often. But he's starting to question things. At the moment we just distract him. Which I know isn't fair. And I know we can't do that forever. The last thing I want is for him to find out by himself. From a friend at school or on the internet. But still I want to wait. What would I say? He's only four. Am I being selfish? It's just that I don't want to talk about it. At all. Ever. It's taken me so long to come to terms with everything myself, I just don't want to put him through it. I know I'm being selfish. The other half of the reason is that talking about everything will give me a relapse. I don't want to go back there. I've been doing so well.

Thank you for your letter. And for trying to explain everything. I think I understand about Flo. I can tell you cared for her and that you did what you thought was right. I can't pretend to understand about what happened afterwards though. It makes no sense at all to me. I have so many questions. Because the man who did those things is not the man I remember. What happened to you? Perhaps it's true that alongside all of us is someone else. Us again, but not quite us. But to answer your question, as a general rule, yes, I think people can change and I do believe in second chances. I don't know how that works on a personal level though. I mean, when you know the people involved. Feelings change everything. I'm sorry. You'd probably like a deeper response. That's all I can manage at the moment.

But there is one letter that I always read in full. I've stuck it in the bottom-right-hand corner so I know where it is. It never moves. I like it more than all the others. This is what it says:

Hello,

We have been watching over your daughter for many years. She is our favourite human being in the world. She is happy. We think you should know that. She has a wonderful family who love her very much and whom she loves very much as well. We sneak into their home sometimes when they're not looking and all we hear is laughter. They have a dog. Just like you used to. They have called him Ronnie. He knows when we're there. He is the only

Alan Feldberg

one who does. We tickle the hair in his ears and he barks at us. They think he wants to be fed or to be let out. They have no idea.

She is worried about you though. She lies in bed and thinks about how you are. She is confused by what happened. And she is a little scared by it. But she loves you so much still. She believes that good things never disappear. That they remain good no matter what comes afterwards.

So, we're writing to you now to let you know that things will be all right. We want you to know that you're our second favourite human being, no matter what you've done, and that she has forgiven you. She misses you and is waiting for you.

Love Chantal, Queen of all the Fairies

Chapter Forty
Now

A bolt slides sideways and a gate opens, but I don't walk through it. For many years I longed for this moment. Then I feared it would never come. Then I feared it would. I am an old man. I don't belong out there. It's not my world anymore.

I no longer think about what I've done. I ran out of new thoughts about it long ago. Simply, I did it. I did those things. I can't explain why. I could justify it once. Not now. They seem to me the actions of a madman. Is that what rehabilitation is? I have learned to live with it. With myself. That is all.

I step forward before I am fully ready. The gate closes immediately behind me and I stand on the empty pavement looking both ways. I don't know what for. The road is lined with small trees, not much taller than twice my height. They have been planted an equal distance apart and somewhere in my brain I acknowledge and appreciate the symmetry. I look upward. I have missed the sky. I have seen it of course, but it is different out here. Different mainly in its unhindered expanse. There is nothing up there at all. Nothing solid. Just wide openness.

I walk towards the nearest tree and under it. It is cool in the shade. The contrast is stark and sends a shiver snaking down my spine. They are lime trees. I can smell the sharp citrus in my nostrils. I pull one off the branch and rub it against my face. A single sob splutters out of me, but I gather myself before I am overwhelmed. And now I wait. Something will happen. Something always happens. No. Not that again. I am different now. I look each way down the road again. For unexplained reasons I expect something horrible to come around the corner at any moment. I don't know what the horrible thing will look like.

On the opposite side of the road a woman is standing on the pavement looking at me. She is in the open. Where was she before? But she's not a woman at all. She's me. A different version of me. I know her. I don't know her. She is a stranger. I know her name.

She begins to say something, but as she does so a car passes between us. The driver has their window down and snatches of song catch in the wind and then vanish. She has stopped talking now. I want to know what she said. I want to say something back. An ocean of words pours in and I can't tell them apart. It's impossible to capture the lost decades in a single sentence. She turns and walks away.

The sob I suppressed a moment ago returns. It is more powerful now. It overcomes me. It forces me back against the tree and I slide down its trunk until I'm sitting at its base. I don't know why I'm crying. My reasons are like the words; there are just too many to identify just one.

'Daddy?'

I can't look at her. I have done wrong things. She is touching my shoulder now. I can't look at her. I think of all the ways in which I misrepresented myself. I was a superhero. I could walk on water. Her hand is reaching down to take mine. She is pulling me to my feet. I still can't look at her. I turn my face away. Our shadows are flat and still on the pavement. There is a gap between them. Not a wide gap. The gap closes and now there is just one shadow.

Day 8,379.

THE END

A note from the publisher

Thank you for reading this book. If you enjoyed it please do consider leaving a review on Amazon to help others find it too.

We hate typos. All of our books have been rigorously edited and proofread, but sometimes mistakes do slip through. If you have spotted a typo, please do let us know and we can get it amended within hours.

info@bloodhoundbooks.com

Milton Keynes UK
Ingram Content Group UK Ltd.
UKHW010925230124
436525UK00007B/144

9 781916 978485